Florida Gothic Stories

Florida Gothic Stories

Vicki Hendricks

Florida Gothic Stories

Second printing 2014

Winona Woods Books
5660 Winona Trail
De Leon Springs, FL 32130

Library of Congress Control Number: 2009941634

Cover photo: ©Clyde Butcher, www.clydebutcher.com
Back cover portrait: Garry Kravit

Florida Gothic Stories is a work of fiction. Names, characters, places, and incidents are the products of the author's imagination or are used fictitiously. Any resemblance to actual events, locales, or persons, living or dead, is entirely coincidental.

*For all the crazed inhabitants of Florida—
my inspiration in paradise*

Acknowledgements

For every word of fiction that I have ever written, I am grateful to the faculty of the Creative Writing Department of Florida International University, especially James W. Hall, Les Standiford, and most of all, Lynne Barrett, who continues to be my mentor.

I am also deeply appreciative to Anne Petty for her labor of love in creating Kitsune Books, and in particular, for publishing my collection. I am sincerely indebted to Megan Abbott and Michael Connelly for an introduction and an afterword of incredible elegance and praise. More appreciation and delight go to Clyde Butcher for the use of his stunning photograph "Loosescrew Gator." I only hope that my stories are worthy to be surrounded by such talent.

Final thanks to Brian Sullivan, who is my first reader as well as my instant thesaurus and encyclopedia—faster than Google.

I gratefully acknowledge the original editors and publishers of my stories:

• "West End," in *Murder for Revenge*, ed. Otto Penzler, Delacorte.

• "ReBecca," on *nerve.com*, ed. Genevieve Field; also in *Best American Erotica 2000*, edited by Susie Bright, Simon & Schuster.

- "Gators," on *mississippireview.com*, ed. A. Neil Smith; also in *Flesh and Blood: Erotic Tales of Crime and Passion*, eds. Max Allan Collins and Jeff Gelb, Warner Books.
- "Stormy, Mon Amour," in *Tart Noir*, eds. Stella Duffy and Lauren Henderson, Berkeley Prime Crime.
- "Boozanne, Lemme Be," in *Miami Noir*, ed. Les Standiford, Akashic Books.
- "The Big O," in *A Hell of a Woman: An Anthology of Female Noir*, ed. Megan Abbott, Busted Flush Press.
- "Sweet Dreams," in Florida International University's *Gulf Stream Magazine*, no. 28, eds. Denise Lanier and Joe Clifford.
- "Must Bite!" in *Dying For It: Tales of Sex and Death*, ed. Mitzi Szereto, Thunder's Mouth Press; also in *The Erotic Treasury*, ed. Susie Bright, Chronicle Books.
- "Sinny and the Prince," in *Murdaland: Crime Fiction for the 21st Century*, no. 2, ed. Michael Lagnas.

Table of Contents

Introduction by Megan Abbott • 10

Stormy, *Mon Amour* • 14
Boozanne, Lemme Be • 35
ReBecca • 54
Must Bite! • 67
Cold-Blooded Lovers • 93
Gators • 112
M-F Dog • 131
The Big O • 146
West End • 169
Sinny and the Prince • 183
Sweet Dreams • 201

Afterword by Michael Connelly • 224

Introduction

by Megan Abbott

"The mosquitoes thicken with the night," says the narrator of Vicki Hendricks' "Stormy, *Mon Amour*," "but finally the moon comes up like a mother-of-pearl saucer, lighting my heart with hope and courage."

The line is vintage Vicki Hendricks—capturing the desperate sincerity of so many of her characters. In another writer's hand, the fact that the narrator's object of desire is a dolphin named Stormy would be the garish punchline, but Hendricks lifts these strange and damaged characters—elevates their helpless clambering and errant desires to the level of high drama.

This line, with its sudden burst of guilelessness and innocence ("lighting my heart with hope and courage"), dances just to the edge of pulp kitsch but never teeters over. Instead, it echoes those sweeping, sad moments in James M. Cain, when murderous protagonists offer us fleeting glimpses into the purest part of their wayward hearts. "I kissed her," the narrator of *The Postman Always Rings Twice* tells us. "Her eyes were shining up at me like two blue stars. It was like being in church" (Vintage, 1992, 17). These lines, the twinge they send through us in spite (and because) of the tabloid depravity that forms the scaffolding of these stories—why, it's such an art—all the more because it is so lightly rendered—and Hendricks is its contemporary master.

These stories—they're raw and beautiful creations that summon up the world of not only Cain, but Jim Thompson, Horace McCoy, Charles Willeford. But they are not gritty tales, and they are not hardboiled. They're too strange and haunted for that. You don't feel like you're touching the real when you read them; you feel like you're touching—no, drowning—in something more real than real. Expressionistic mindscapes of desire, sorrow and need. While the doomfulness of noir snakes through every story here, it's not the heart beating at the center.

The collection's title gives the clue. These are stories suffused with the southern gothic tradition. Not Faulkner so much as Flannery O'Connor, Carson McCullers— characters that teeter or tilt to sideshow but then, through Hendricks's nimble touch and the affection she has for every lost soul, become sad, even poignant figures who occasionally, as in the case of Mouse, the diminutive narrator of "Boozanne, Lemme Be," rise to the level of mock heroic. With each twist of the knife in these stories, you feel their pain, rough and hapless.

Frequently, Hendricks's work is singled out for its erotic intensity, and we see it in these stories too. But it would be a mistake to see these as salacious tales. Rather, sex is currency in the stories, and it's a tool, especially for the women, but most of all it's a way of reaching out for something, anything. And it's a way of hanging on. "We both began to laugh," the narrator of "M-F Dog" tells us, "We shook and howled and guffawed, holding each other

by the shoulders, until all the loneliness of my lifetime
tumbled down and disappeared between the cushions
of the ugly couch, like small change. We couldn't stop
snuffing and snorting, and the sounds of our laugher sent
us into high abandon. She stripped off her shirt—as if it
would help her breathe—and her tits burst brighter than
sunset..." Sex is a balm here, a bulwark against the world.
It can also, of course, prove the shortest distance to the
gallows, but the aim is pure. Sex is the promise of rescue, if
just for a moment, from everything else.

First and foremost, these are desperate characters,
and we see that piercingly reading them back to back,
following each character as he or she surrenders to the
worst impulses, and then pays the price. We may even
feel smug as we read of their abasement, tsk-tsk at their
greed. But then Hendricks always turns the screw. Time
and again, the struggling protagonists, dreaming their big
dreams, face aftermaths almost too horrible to bear—and
their final thoughts are about, alternately, surrender and
survival.

"Like the snap of a bone, his laugh shot chills up my
spine and the sorry truth to my brain. I was the same as
Carl, only he'd been desperate all his life. My damned arm
would be second to go. I'd already handed Satan my soul."

"It was like being caught under a wave, but I knew I
was dreaming, so I didn't struggle. My luck was changing. I
just had to hold my breath till the sun came out."

"I pictured [her] down the block, big and bold as she
was, sticking out her thumb, and a gold Cadillac stopping,
its doors opening like wings, to fly her away."

The last lines to these stories lift the veil and we
suddenly see we're not talking about chumps and gold-

diggers and losers. We're not talking about shallow souls getting their comeuppance. We're talking about longing and mystery and freedom and even, sometimes, holy redemption.

Ultimately, these endings are fingers pointed at us. Who are we to judge these damaged souls, who rise higher than we do because, in the end, they care more, need more, grasp for it, because, for them, everything matters so much? These are dreamers, yearners, and even in their pettiest desires—for revenge, for the dollar, for sexual adventure —they are beautiful. In Hendricks' tender hands, they are beautiful.

—Megan Abbott, October 4, 2009

Stormy, *Mon Amour*

It's a breach birth, and soon as I see the tail slip out between my legs, I know I am caught. The doctors start to mumble about fixing "her deformity"—"replace rubbery gray hide with skin grafts" . . . "sculpt feet from the finlike appendage" . . . "separate muscles and bones to create legs." But I'm filled with pride and wonder at her beauty—and how I widened the gene pool. "Don't touch her," I tell them. "She's perfect."

Roger figures it out on the way home from the hospital. "Jesus Christ!" he screams. "It's Stormy's, isn't it? You fucked that dolphin! You fucked that dolphin!" He glares into my eyes, and I can only worry about him keeping the car on the road.

"Only you, Cherie," he says. "Only a fuckin' French bimbo like you would think you could pass it off as my kid. I always said you'd fuck a snake—but fuck a fish? Christ." He stares straight ahead. His hands are bloodless on the steering wheel.

"He's a warm-blooded mammal," I tell him. "He loves me."

I sit back and look out the window. Roger shakes his head and makes a hissing noise between his teeth, and in my mind, I'm outta there. I'm sick of him telling me to use my brains instead of my heart, to "Grow up, grow up, grow up." He must have told me a million times that the world is a tough place and I better get used to it. He says I'd be found dead on the highway if he wasn't around to protect me. But, to me, the only one I need protecting from is Roger. Before I got pregnant he smacked me hard enough to put a tooth through my lip, and one time he dislocated my shoulder. He was so sorry I forgave him, but now I have a daughter to think about.

"Well, Cherie, I'm not stupid enough to support that fucking fish and let her father off the hook. Get your stringy little blonde French ass outta here. Take that thing and hit the road, before somebody finds out."

I don't bother to mention that she is a mammal also, a mermaid—or to explain how I fell in love with a dolphin. Roger is mumbling how he'd rather see the likes of her on a platter, but I ignore him, the swine. He's making it easy for me because I hate him more now than over the whole three years we've been married.

He wants me out by the weekend—tells me to charge a flight to my mother's in Quebec. But I figure the next day when he's at the restaurant, I'll hop a Greyhound for Islamorada. Asshole owns the car. All the time I'm asking myself why I handed my life over to a pudgy forty-year-old redneck who cooks animal flesh for a living. When I hitchhiked out of Canada, I never expected to become a redneck myself, a country girl in the sticks of Central Florida, taught everything by Roger. Now I'm twenty-one, legal, and have all the courage of a new mother to make a life for myself and my baby. I don't care about the rest of the world and what they might think about me and Stormy. We understand each other, and that's it. He trusts

my judgment with every rubbery inch of his slick hard
body, and with that to hang onto, I can make it work.

The next morning I wrap Mineaux's fin in a diaper and
a wet blanket and slide her bottom into a plastic Winn-
Dixie sack, so she's moist and comfortable for the long
bus ride. The hundred bucks I've saved is in the diaper
bag alongside canned tuna and sardines I scrounged from
the pantry. It's a short walk to the station, and we're on
the bus in no time. I know exactly where to find the new
father. He was taken out of the show for sexual behavior
toward the female swimmers—really just me—and put in
the isolation lagoon, where he had to learn tricks for his
supper. I've been suffering with love ever since, and I can't
wait to see him. Love, *mon dieu*. No stopping it. There's a
legend that pink dolphins in Peru change themselves into
human shape to seduce the village girls, make them fall
in love. The dolphins wear hats made from dried fruit to
cover their blowholes. Stormy never needed a hat.

I nurse Mineaux every time she wakes, napping in
between until Key Largo. Then I hold her up to see the
shining water, my eyes searching for dolphins from every
bridge, even though I know he's not there. It's a beautiful
place to start a fresh life. I get a cab from the bus station to
Theater of the Sea. I'm not sure how to sneak Minny and
me into the pool with Stormy, and I have a few days to heal
before I can get into the water, but at least I can show him
his new daughter.

It's four o'clock when I walk through the gate. Only
an hour left. I step right up to the window and charge
the admission on Visa. I hope Roger hasn't thought of
canceling. I tell them I don't want to swim, but they still
make me pay to get inside. It's expensive. I wonder how

long till I can get a job. Childcare might be a problem.

My spirits rise at a glimpse of Stormy's lagoon. I nearly skip across the concrete down the path to the grass at the edge of the pool where I last saw him. There are no shows going on and no Theater employees in sight. I search the surface of the water for the roll of his shiny gray head or a snort from his blowhole. I'm starting to worry he's been taken away when I catch a glimpse of him gliding along the glassy edge. He's fast and sleek. Sunlight glints off his head and makes him shine like mercury as he rolls and sinks. I'm not sure if he's seen me, but I'm in awe of his perfection and can't break the moment.

When his head emerges at the far side of the pool, I greet him with the series of squeaks I've learned. We don't understand each other's signals exactly, but the specifics aren't important.

Stormy dives under and makes a run. He surfaces in front of me and flings a set of drips off his nose that glint in the setting sun. I recognize his mannerisms. He's full of glee. I hold Minny to my side and squat on my heels as his gray vinyl face looms up. I tilt forward to touch him with my cheek. He catches the scent of the baby and sinks slowly back into the water, holding there without the flicker of a fin, his eyes bright and level with the bundle in my arms. I gently unwrap Minny, who is sleeping through all this, and set her down on the smooth rock edge in front of him. Her upper body skin is pink and soft, but her tail is thick tough hide, the best combination of both Stormy and me. She opens her eyes and begins to squirm. The black in Stormy's eyes deepens. I can feel his love and wonder welling up around us.

We're the perfect family, even if a photograph wouldn't

show it. He nudges Minny with his beak, and I think he wants me to put her into the lagoon beside him. It worries me, in case I'm misinterpreting his intentions. I look at his upturned face, his snout making an upward jerking motion, same as when he wants fish, but there's love in his eyes, unmistakable. He knows he's the father and he wants to see her. He holds still a little ways out, in the calm lapping of wavelets. I lower her slowly and put her tail into the water a few inches. She isn't used to the temperature. Her fin pulls up and she looks at me with a scrunched face and starts to cry. I gather her, wet tail dripping against my body, and look around to make sure we're still safe.

Stormy hovers impatiently. "Just wait a few days, *mon amour*," I tell him. I'm afraid. I want to be able to get in with her. I know he's hurting for a touch, but I rewrap her. She's so tiny, and he can be a little rough. She squirms and nuzzles to nurse, so I slip my shirt up and she goes at it while Stormy watches with a father's love. I know how much he wants to flop up on the grass beside us, and he has the strength to do it, but he holds back. When Minny dozes off, I set her down behind me, with the blanket bunched up under her head to keep her comfortable, and crawl back to the edge. I lie down so my head is close to the water. Stormy has been watching from somewhere under the surface and he rises up and rubs his face against mine over and over like a cat, only more primitive, and stronger. I ache to get in the water with him. Ever since I met him that's where I always want to be.

I put my arms over his round, smooth shoulder area and hold him, touch one finger to the rim of his blowhole, and stroke it gently like he enjoys. The sun is low and the air still. Minny is peaceful. I could be happy to stay like this forever.

"Park closing" blares on the loudspeaker and startles me. I sit up and glance around, but there's nobody in sight. I dry my arms on my shorts as Stormy watches from a few feet out. He waits there and I blow him a kiss, pick up Minny, and walk back along the path. I look over my shoulder every few steps so he knows I really don't want to leave.

I have to be careful, so I bring Mineaux back only once in the first week. I don't put her in the water, although she already takes an interest in it and reaches out toward Stormy. "Pa Pa," I tell her. "That's your Pa Pa."

Lucky for me, right away I get a job at Lorelei's down the road. It's a nice dockside restaurant with a giant mermaid out front to attract attention—a colossal Mineaux. I move out of the motel I've been charging and into a tiny apartment across the street from the restaurant, for rent by the week. Lorelei's agrees to let me work lunch and early afternoon. People are nice in the Keys. That way I can leave Minny during her nap and get a free meal a day, besides saving enough tips to pay the rent. My only expenses are diapers, the admission to see Stormy, and a little food. I don't like leaving my baby alone, but she sleeps sound and I can't think what else to do. Two times the next week, I get her up after work and walk her over to see her papa. It's all the life I need.

After two weeks I feel safe to get into the water. I have no way to tell Stormy why I haven't joined him sooner, but it's one of those things he accepts on trust. Never a complaint out of him. On the first night, I wear my bathing suit under my shorts, and when I stand and peel off the shorts, he lets out a throat full of wild high-pitched

whoops. I have a little extra stomach on me, but one of
the best things about Stormy is that he always thinks I'm
beautiful. I slide next to him in the cool water, and for the
first time since the day we met, I wrap my arms around
his body, the supple hardness no man can compete with.
He's able to change the texture of his hide according to
his mood, and he turns himself into velvet, sliding around
and nudging across me with his catlike grace. He puts his
erection under my arm—a touch like chamois over steel.
He tows me around in his circles of glee until I get dizzy
and let go.

I want to take off my suit, but I don't dare. If Minny
starts to cry, someone might hear, and the staff will come
running. I have to be quick. I hug that thick smooth hide
and cling to Stormy's satin underbelly, my thighs gripping
the curve of his back, feet locked over his side fins. He
nuzzles me and brings out his flat gray tongue, letting it
rest partially out of his mouth. I twist around his head,
swiping his tongue across my shoulders, sending tingles
down my back. I yank my top down and lower myself until
his mouth and tongue are nearly swallowing my chest, the
touch of smooth rubber and fine suede. I fasten myself
tighter against him, feeling the hot rush I've longed for.

I glance behind me. We're at the far end of the spit
of land and so far nobody has wandered back after the
last show, but it's still a risk. I find his erection with my
foot and rush his foreplay. It's a spike I can stand on with
no problem, but I have no fear when I pull my bottoms
aside and slip myself down over it as he rises under me,
stretching me to my limit. He lies on his back to let me
take control and holds level in the water while I work
myself up and back, my own moisture making me more

slippery than he is. The water warms up around us with the heat of our feelings. I hold him close, my face near his huge clear eye, like a crystal ball, as I feel the orgasm building inside my whole body. Sky and water blend into a sparkling blur. Stormy is still, tilted in the water, his tail waving slowly under us to keep my head above the surface, while I stay locked around him and float in a daze against his pure gray body.

Voices coming from down the path shock me back into the world. I scramble to get out, dress, and pick up Mineaux. A man and woman smile as they come to stand beside us and gaze at Stormy in his pool. They have no idea what they missed, but I'm shivering and feeling the effects of a lucky escape.

A month passes fast. Stormy and me are the happiest couple I can imagine. Minny has grown double the size expected for a normal baby, and I feel safe to put her in the water. It's July, plenty warm, and one night I dip her fin to the hips. Her face shows surprise, but I make happy noises until she coos. Then I lower her waist-deep, level with Stormy's face on the surface. He nudges her side like a kitten, and she puts her pink baby fingers flat against his skin. He makes a soft squeak in his throat and she answers him with a noise I can't imitate. She smiles. It's an instant connection. "Mineaux loves her papa," I tell him. He hovers there, not making a sound, but his eyes are keen on her. We're just like a real family, except there's no yelling, no hitting, and no money problems to worry about. I glance behind me. Nobody watching.

I hold my breath and dip her face. She screeches, blinks, and opens her eyes wide as I bring her up. Instinct kicks in. Her arms flap and her tail pulsates so strong I can

barely hold her. Stormy nudges my arm and I know he's
saying to let her go. I'm not ready so soon, but I can't let
them miss this moment. I take a breath, ready to plunge
in beside her, and let go of her waist. She takes off on a
straight path just under the surface of the water. Her arms
streamline to her sides and she pumps to her own rhythm
across the lagoon. Stormy is stunned for a second, but then
he's by her side, gliding and watching as she surfaces for air,
her face glowing with a baby smile I know isn't caused by
gas. They begin to play, circling each other, Stormy letting
out his most joyous shrieks and Mineaux rising up like an
angel from the water to stand on her tail beside her father.
They race in the glow of sunset. My heart is bursting with
love. I'm straining over the edge, enjoying their special
bonding, and there's only the slightest pinch in my heart
because I can never share in their world completely.

I get in. They help me to overcome some of my human
weakness in the water, holding me between their sturdy
skins at the right angle for a smooth ride. I learn to pulse
my legs and keep up with the help of a tiny arm on one
side and a fin on the other.

Our lives would be a fantasy come true, if we didn't
have to beware of the rest of the world. As I take Minny
out of the water, I see the sadness in Stormy's face, the
slight downturn of his mouth. The scary thought that he
wants me to leave her with him runs through my head. I
know that he must be lonely and unhappy doing tricks all
day for his food in that small lagoon, and we are the only
part of his life he cares about. He's beginning to look lean
and pale, even though he always has that built-in dolphin
smile. His eyes are dull and his head is breaking out in
small bumps. I know that dolphins can commit suicide by

closing their blowholes and refusing to breathe, and I'm
worried. He's suffering. I read it in his eyes that he wants
her there, but I can't leave her.

I'm walking past the office with Minny on my hip,
headed to the exit, when a man steps out in front of me.
He has a mean look on his face, and I know he's seen me
several times. I'm sure there's been talk from the staff about
my hanging around. I make the choice to defy him even
before he can get any words out.

"I'm reporting you to the police," I say. "You've got
a dolphin in here against his will, and that's cruelty to
animals."

He shakes his head and frowns. "We've had nuts like
you here before—cutting our gate, trying to free the
dolphins. The police are on our side."

I hold Minny tight against me. "I belong to FETA," I
say. "We're not well known like PETA, but we protect the
fish in this universe. We're tough."

"Dolphins aren't fish," he says. He walks past me
laughing.

"I know that," I yell. "We protect them too."

He looks back at me and his eyebrows go up, like
he thought he heard words come out of my mouth, but
decided it was only mosquito buzz. I turn toward the
exit to get out of there with the baby. Right then a light
comes on in my brain. It's a dim nightlight, but there's
enough glow to see that all my life I've been a push-over,
somebody to ignore or boss around, and it's my own
damn fault. I never stand up for myself, just run away from
trouble and get nowhere. I've spent the last two months
living like Stormy was going to rise up on his hind fin and
swoop me over some threshold and into my dream world.

But it's up to me to make a life for myself, my lover, and my daughter. Soon I'm going to get caught, and if they find out about Mineaux, she could become a test subject—a million bad things could happen.

I watch the guy as he goes into the office. If he reports me I'll get banned from the grounds. I have a feeling there's going to be trouble, and I need to get Stormy out of there before I get cut off or his condition gets worse. I think he's sick with sadness that comes from seeing what life could be for us if we had our freedom. He's helpless and hopeless.

Roger would say, "Put your blonde brain into overdrive." The memory spurs me with a plan to beat them all. There's just one chain link fence that separates Stormy from the open water, and all I have to do is cut a dolphin-size hole. Then I can follow him down the Keys and find a new place to stay where he's free to visit whenever he wants and roam the ocean like he's supposed to naturally. For the first time in my life I realize that sometimes it's right to break the law. Tonight is the full moon, my best chance, for reasons of light and luck, to get him out.

I quit at Lorelei's and tell them I'm sorry. I have no choice. I'll call about my check in a week. I'm ready to cry, so they don't ask questions. I leave at four and cross the street to my apartment. I'm in a nervous hurry, because I have to rent a kayak before the guy closes, and then take a taxi to rent the bolt cutters. I put my key into the door to unlock it, but it locks instead. It seems I forgot to lock when I ran over during my break. I turn the key back and step inside panicky, realizing that Minny has been there for a couple hours when anyone could walk in.

Roger is sitting in the big chair by the window. He looks rougher than ever, with white stubble on his chin

and his gray hair grown into a skinny ponytail. He's
smoking a cigarette. A Bud is on the table next to him.

"*Merde*," I say. "Fuck."

"Cherie, baby. I'm here to take care of you, honey."

My hands are shaking and I hold the door half open,
dreaming that he could possibly slither back out. I'm
unable to run because of Minny in the bedroom, but I
don't want to shut myself in with him. He stands up, walks
over, and slams the door.

"How'd you get inside, Roger?"

He goes back to the chair. "What's a matter,
sweetheart? I want to forgive and forget. I can't live
without my little honey. I'm fallin' apart without you,
babe."

I dart down the hall, not taking my eyes off him until
I'm out of sight. I check on Minny. She's sleeping sound
and her diaper and blanket are still wet inside the plastic
bag. I close the door to the bedroom and take a big breath
before dragging myself back to the living room. All I can
think about is that I have less than an hour to get rid of him
and rent the boat and the bolt cutters.

"How'd you find me?"

"Pooh. I knew you were here since you used that Visa
card. Where else would you go anyway?"

I shrug.

"I wasn't thinking right when I told you to leave, baby-
doll. It's not like you cheated on me with another man."
He laughs and shakes his head, but his eyes are flat. "This
is special. It's a beautiful thing. We'll never have to work
again. We've got a genetic miracle here, and they'll pay us
big bucks and fly us all over the world. The kid'll be famous
and so will we."

I sit down on the rattan couch. All I can think is to fuck him fast and send him off to some bar. He isn't going to leave until he gets it and feels back in control. We did the split-up routine a couple times during the marriage, and I didn't have the sense to stay gone. Roger will figure I'm sucker enough to try us again. Then he'll be happy to head to the next beer light down the road. Me and Minny will go south with Stormy—maybe all the way to the Dry Tortugas if that's what it takes never to see Roger again. I don't like cheating on Stormy, but it's my only choice, and since he can't ask questions, I'll never have to lie.

I smile and sit down on Roger's lap. His human stench closes around me and I throw my head to his shoulder and fake a gag into a sob. "Hold me, big honey, I've been so lonely."

It's a nauseating idea to touch Roger's foul mouth, but I concentrate on closing off my senses and becoming a machine. He takes me into his grisly hairy arms and pulls my head back to start sucking at my lips. I taste the hot sick slime of human spit passed from him to me, and I dig my nails into his back to brace myself while he sucks and slurps. He smears his sloppy tongue and lips over my face, until I feel clammy. He crams my mouth full of his tongue so the sharp bite of cigarettes stings the back of my throat. Beer burps thicken the air I breathe. I try to think of salty spray. I'll bathe myself inside and out before I ever touch Stormy and expose him to foul, infected human mucus.

There isn't much time, so I swallow my disgust, pull my shirt over my head, and step out of my shorts. Roger wedges off his shoes, toe to heel, and I squat to unbutton his shirt while he yanks off his socks. As fast as I can, I slip the shirt off his shoulders, unhook his belt, and rip down his pants. He's ready to go, as big and hard as most humans can get. I put my legs around him, sit down on his purplish cock, and work myself up and down, applying all the pressure I'm able so he can't hold out for long.

"Oh, yeah, that's my little gal," he drawls. "Yeah, man."

I make some squeaky noises of my own, like I used to, but I'm spoiled by Stormy's fresh fish smell and smooth, thick steel-hard organ. This doesn't even feel like sex to me anymore, much less like anything called love. Roger's skin is hot and squishy and when he starts to sweat I think I'll puke. He's fast, thank God. His ears go red, and he gives out that call like a bull elephant. I don't mean to insult the elephant, but Roger could do sound effects on Discovery. He's in and out of me in less than a minute. His head lolls and he leans back to doze in the chair. I can't leave him there with Minny, and I need to lock up and get a move on.

I tug his hand. "Hon, I have to go back to work. There's a nice place down the road where you can wait for me. Beer's much cheaper than across the street at Lorelei's— almost free. Unless you want to stay here and watch Minny? She might wake up with a dirty diaper and then you could change her for me and give her some sardines."

He opens his eyes and lets his jaw drop, then makes a smacking noise in his jowls. "I'll take your first suggestion, Toots. I'm pretty thirsty after that workout. Mmm, mmm. You're still one sweet little thing."

His ass rises off the couch in an instant, like I figured it would at the mention of childcare, and he pulls on his clothes as fast as I've seen him move when his burgers were burning on the grill. I watch him walk down the sidewalk and he makes a turn into the driveway where a car is parked. It's a new one. He's been spending money, probably counting on Minny as a gold mine.

I put on my clothes and check her. She's sound asleep and I can only pray she stays like that. I take the two-day's tips I've saved and my laundry quarters and my driver's license, in case they require some kind of security. It's a hot walk the short distance to the kayak rental, and I sweat my way down the street, moisture pouring off me from rushing and planning a lie. No other way. I can't move Stormy before dark, so I'll have to rent the kayak for an hour and steal it, at least temporarily. It's the only way I can get to the gate and cut it. I never did anything like this before.

It's a young guy, smoking some herb, and he lets me pay for one hour and takes my expired driver's license as a deposit without even looking at it. It has my right name, but I intend to bring back the kayak the next day anyway. I take my life preserver and get in and paddle out of sight of the rental guy, to a piece of land alongside the park, on the other side of the fence. I tie up to the overhanging mangroves, nice camouflage. I just have to take a chance that nobody will wander over there and take the boat. A lot left to fate, but I have confidence because I'm doing the right thing.

I walk back to the road and cross to the Tom Thumb grocery. I call a taxi and wait. It's only 5:30, so I'm okay so far. The time stretches to 5:50 by the time the cab pulls in, and I'm getting frantic thinking of how long this is going to take, Minny all alone, and Roger less than half a mile away.

I tell the driver to wait while I go into the rental place for the cutters. Behind the desk the man looks at me odd, like he knows I'm up to something, but it's the Keys after all, so he doesn't say anything. I fill out a form and leave

the Visa as a deposit. I don't know if I'll be able to return
the cutters, so Roger will have to take care of the bill when
it comes. Lucky for me he decided to make his fortune
on Minny and never canceled my credit. If it wasn't for
Catholic school upbringing, I could have used the card
plenty to my advantage, but those nuns just never let loose.
I feel them grabbing at my ankles now, even as I keep on
moving in what I know is the right direction in the long
run.

The taxi driver turns to look, but I drag the bolt cutters
onto the seat and tell him to take me back to the Tom
Thumb. I think he's on to me, too, but I don't give a rat's
ass, as long as he doesn't stop me. I have him drop me near
the path to the water. I hand him my last four dollars and
change, and it barely makes the fare. He hands me a dollar
back. "You might need this, girlie."

I smile and thank him. I can't do much with a dollar,
but it's good will, and that pumps up my heart with hope
and brightens my face into a smile as I swing the bolt
cutters onto my shoulder and shut the door.

I walk the short distance to where I tied the kayak and
smear my arms and legs with jungle-strength Deet to scare
away the mosquitoes. I climb into the plastic boat and drag
the cutters from shore and plunk them between my legs.
At this moment it occurs to me that I might not be strong
enough to cut the chain link fence that jails Stormy. I have
no idea how much muscle it'll take. But I have no choice. I
tell myself I can do it. I will do it. It's right.

I dip my paddles and ease out on the silvery surface,
following my long skinny shadow over dark water where
grasses grow and unfriendly sea creatures are lurking. I
have maybe a mile to paddle around the point and into the

area of the manmade lagoon where Stormy is captive. The last rays of the sun are warm on my back and I glide slowly, not wanting to reach the gate until dark. My mind is racing with thoughts of Roger so nearby and Minny probably awake by now, hungry and wet with urine that could turn her slick hide to dull gray blisters, her version of diaper rash.

I reach the edge of Stormy's lagoon while it's still light and tie up under the mangroves to wait. The mosquitoes thicken with the night, but finally the moon comes up like a mother-of-pearl saucer, lighting my heart with courage. I make my way to the chain-link barrier where my love waits. I hear his blow three times before I see him. He senses my presence on the other side of the spit of land and waits, probably wondering why I never came to visit at the usual time and place.

As I round the corner to the high-fenced area, he rears up and looks me in the eye through the links. I reach two fingers inside and caress his silky nose and purse my lips to kiss the smooth tip. Under his gaze, I lift the bolt cutters, which are heavy just to hold, and put the pinch on a piece of chain-link at surface level. I use all my strength, squeezing the handles hard and getting nowhere. I take a breath—one, two, three—a hard punch, all I've got. I feel the blades bite, and the link snaps. I'm ecstatic, yet there are many more to go. I'll need to cut a big door to peel the fence back far enough for Stormy to swim through, but now that I've done one link, there's no stopping me.

I crouch low in the kayak to get the right angle, resting after each effort, but working myself into a sweat fast. It takes all my strength each time, and my arm muscles are shaking by the time I'm a third of the way finished. I can't

let Stormy see, but I'm crying silently. I'm worn down and
sick with fear thinking of Minny at home and it's nearly
midnight. I can only hope Roger found some drinking
buddies to keep him out late. It's the Keys, I remind myself,
so that's a given.

I have to get into the water as I work lower, taking
breaths and going under when my arms can't reach. I'm
cold and shivering, even though the water temperature is
probably way above 80. Finally, I make the last necessary
cut and try to bend open the door I've created. It's tough.
I climb back into the kayak, wedge its nose into the open
space to widen it, and swing the boat against the cut flap to
crush it against the immovable part of the fence. I smash
the boat into it a few times to make sure the crease will
stay, and Stormy will have plenty of room so not to scratch
himself swimming through. I pull the boat out and back
off, giving him space to make his break for freedom. He
lifts himself to his tail and takes a look through the fence
before making a move.

"Let's go, honey," I whisper. I'm panting from
excitement and exhaustion, my teeth chattering with cold.
I motion with my hand. "Swim through the hole." I know
he doesn't understand my words—not anything he's been
taught—but he can see that his way is clear. I don't know
why he's hesitating. He must not realize that somebody
could find us at any second and close us off forever. I wish I
brought a fish or two to lure him out faster.

Stormy sinks under the water and I think he's ready
to shoot on past—still he waits. His eyes are wide open,
but dull with the ill health that's been creeping over him. I
wonder if I'm too late and he's weak. Or maybe he's scared
to leave his daily portion of dead fish. He hasn't survived

on live fish for years and can't know that I'll keep him supplied. He floats silent and still. His eyes look from me to the hole and back again, but there's no flicker of motion.

I plead. "Sweetheart, go, go, go…. Please. Stormy, *mon amour*, swim…. Come with me. We'll live together—in freedom, *cheri*—with our baby. *Plût à Dieu!*"

I flop off the boat and swim through the opening and grab his top fin. I kick with all my strength and try to pull him forward, but the fluttering of my skinny legs, in comparison to the churning power of his mighty tail, is nothing but sound and splash. I kick and pull and kick until I wear myself out. My face slips underwater. As I lift myself for a breath, I choke, and Stormy puts his fin under my arm and boosts me up. I quit coughing and start to sob. He's not going anywhere, ever. He's too well trained.

I hang there on Stormy, crying and shaking, while he rests solid as a mountain in the wavelets. For the first time I wonder if he has ever shared the hot sharp pain of love between us, the need to be together or die that made me put my soul to the test and rise above my ordinary self to commit this deed. The sudden cold dawn of awareness is terrifying. I want to sink below the surface and stop breathing like he can do, never face the air and the world again. It's clear to me that he has never experienced the passionate longing I've read in his eyes. He has never loved me in human terms—and I am an idiot.

I gain back my senses and realize that I have to go home to Mineaux, but I can barely pull myself into reality. I look for the kayak. It has drifted away. I can't spot it across the vacant moonlit water. The park will be locked if I go out that way, and it's a long walk back around the point to the road, but my only choice. I've stolen the kayak and the bolt cutters and lost them both—I'm a criminal with no money, no reason to live—and a crippled child to care for.

I swim out through the fence and turn back for one last look at Stormy. He's waiting and watching, as he always does when I leave. I don't know what is inside his brain. I never did. I'm freezing and weak, but I breast stroke down the line of fence toward a shallow place where I can climb out. I see moving lights in the distance and figure they're from the road, a road I had hoped to go down and never come back.

One set of lights moves in a different direction, and as I swim, it seems that this might be a car driving toward me on the point of land that I have to walk down. I pass the last piece of fence and climb out onto the rocky edge. It is a car, getting closer. I lower myself back into the water to hide. It must be the police. In a few minutes the car pulls up and stops. There are no beacons, only headlights. I realize the perimeter fence blocks the car from going any farther. The door opens and a man gets out. He walks to the fence and his face catches moonlight—Roger.

He looks into the nearest pool on the other side of the fence and then sits down on the hood. Somehow he knows I'm here. He's planning to wait. I don't know what to do. I can try to swim past him without making a sound and hide in the brush until he drives away. I'm ready to give it a try when I hear crying. Good god. Minny's in the car. I haul my dripping self up the rocks. Roger sees me and stands watching as I take a few steps and stop to cough.

"I knew it," he says. "Blonde French bimbo."

"I need to get the baby, Roger."

"I was in the Tom Thumb buying cigarettes. Saw you get into a taxi with bolt cutters."

"Oh." I twist my hair and wring it behind me, walk past him, and open the car door. Mineaux smiles at me from her baby-seat. I reach for her and hold her against my shivering wet body, taking her warmth, knowing she doesn't feel the cold.

Roger stands looking down at me. "I thought maybe you were picking up tools for your boss, so I went on back to the bar, but I couldn't quit thinking. When I got to your place it was midnight. I knew exactly what you were up to."

He purses his lips and nods his head—like he's so clever, and I'm such a loser. He's half right.

"What kind of a mother are you anyway, leaving your kid all night without food—and nearly dry? I changed her, fed her, and rewet her tail wrap. I don't know what you'd do without me."

I sob into Minny's blanket, with nothing left except the painful knowledge of my lunacy. Roger motions me into his arms, but I turn and scoot into the car and close the door. He gets in and flips on the heat to warm me up. I'm going with him, and that's all he cares about.

Maybe I won't have to share Mineaux with the world, or maybe I should. I don't know what Roger will expect from us, but I know all that Stormy never had to offer.

Minny reaches a finger toward the light of the radio dial and bubbles a baby sound of wonder. I made a big mistake, but I did a damn good job of it.

Boozanne, Lemme Be

I never needed "stuff," so it was easy to live—till Boozanne come along. Most stuff is just to impress women, and I didn't need them either—till Boozanne. I had a cute face—like a puppy dog—I heard, but being four foot-ten, I was too short for normal chicks, too tall for a dwarf. I didn't try to fit in. I could afford a hand job now and then. Did me fine. Keep it simple was my motto. When Danny De Vito retired, maybe I'd head out to Hollywood, but for a young guy like myself, the deal I had going was almost as good—till Boozanne messed me up.

Ma had always told me, if you're gonna steal a VW, might as well steal a Cadillac. Well, Ma had that wrong. A VW would've been the right size for me. But when I got outta prison for stealing the Caddy, I gave up car theft altogether. My home was gone. Ma had passed on, bless her soul—Pop had never been around. Being broke and alone, I hitched down to Florida, remembering how warm it was that winter when Ma and me took a vacation, my best memory as a kid. I met Weasel in Miami, and he's the one told me about this gig. It fit me perfect, even better than a VW.

What you do is find a big old wood house, with two foot of crawling space underneath, and cut a hole in the floor under the bed. Easy, if you measure. Beds are never moved. Weasel burgled his way around the islands, so by the time each hole got discovered, he was long gone. With my carpenter experience, and considering I needed a home more than anything, I went him one better by saving the piece of floor, so I could latch it back in place underneath. No mortgage, no taxes, and free food as long as you're not greedy. Nobody would notice, even if they ran a dust mop over the hardwood, a thing that—I'm telling you—most people never do.

My home with the Lamberts, Bob and Melodie, was walking-distance from the beach, came with *Sports Illustrated* and *Gourmet* subscriptions, cable, big-screen TV, and a cat. They had those wood Bahama shutters that hang down and cover the windows, so nobody could see in, and a carport instead of a garage, so I always knew if either car was home. Thick foliage out to the sidewalk made it easy to sneak around back and go under, though I did most of my crawling in and out in the dark. I had plastic runners and a rug remnant from Goodwill under there, my clothes sealed up in black garbage bags to keep out the bugs, a flashlight, toss pillow, and a *Playboy* to pass the waiting time. I never needed toiletries, like toothpaste, shampoo, or deodorant, cause the Lamberts were well supplied. Didn't shave, or I would've got my own razor. It was like living in a full service motel, except I had to clean up after myself. I was set—till fuckin Boozanne.

Bob and Melodie got home each night at seven or later—depending if they ate out—so I'd drop down the hole around 6:30, crawl out at dark, and head to a cheap local bar, or out on a scrounge, then later to my chair on the beach to doze until it was getting toward dawn, time to head home. I'd picked 'em good—upper-middle-class workaholics, too distracted about their jobs to notice the house much, lotsa loose change and doggie-bag leftovers that they usually tossed into the bin within two days. Somebody might as well enjoy it all. Once in a while, I stuck a pepperoni down my pants at the grocery for extra meat. I didn't take big chances, didn't need much. Any violation would send me back to a cell.

I didn't have to be too careful at the home, as long as I remembered to pick my long black hairs off the pillowcase, go easy on the tidbits and liquor, and wash my lunch dishes. Sometimes, I got sick of looking at Bob's coffee cup that he'd leave on the bathroom sink, and I'd wash that too. I was kind of a dark male Goldilocks, only nicer. I felt friendly toward the Lamberts, seeing that I knew so much about their food tastes, possessions, and living habits. Melodie was like the sister I never had, little and dark haired, big eyed and innocent in her pictures. I felt protective toward her. Bob was like an older brother I could live without.

One day, she came home early—I was lucky the lunch dishes were done—and I was in the living room to see the car pull in. I barely made it out the hole. She ran in and tossed herself on the bed and wailed. Her sobs broke my heart while I laid under there listening. I had to stuff my face into my pillow not to make a whimper. I thought maybe her ma had died. After that, all signs of Melly disappeared for most of a week. Her black dresses were gone, and there were tons of used Kleenex in the wastebasket in her bathroom. She had her period on top of it all, so I hoped no cramps. Eventually, from the sympathy cards, I figured out it was her pop that died.

Trying to be of some help, I dusted, wiped out the
refrigerator, vacuumed, and cleaned the toilets for her
while she was gone. Bob didn't go to the funeral, and I
knew he wouldn't take over the cleaning neither. I couldn't
do anything obvious, but I just thought she'd feel better
if the place somehow didn't seem to get dirty—and the
refrigerator needed cleaning bad. Bob was your regular
slob and never noticed nothin'.

Melly brought home some mementos from her father,
his fishing license and a pin from the Marines, so I knew
they were close. I admired the old fella, seeing he probably
enjoyed life and had guts. I found these heavy dark blue
folders right after that, sitting in plain view on the desk. I
thought they were books at first, but when I opened 'em
up, they smelled musty and were filled with U.S. silver
dollars in little slots marked with the years, the real silver
dollars that this country don't make anymore. I could
tell by looking at the edges. I didn't know what they were
worth, but there were close to four hundred of 'em, and a
few from way back in the 30's. I wondered if Melodie knew
the value. I wished I could warn her to put 'em in a safety
deposit box, in case of burglars, like the Weasel.

I buddied up with their cat too. He liked his water
freshened a couple times a day, and he would have starved
while Melodie was gone if I wasn't there to refill his dry
food. I really performed a service. He was smart, and I
taught him to give paw and roll over for Whisker Lickin's,
tuna-flavored treats. I hid the packet in the empty cabinet
above the refrigerator, and I had to laugh every time I
pictured the Lamberts finding it and being downright
stumped. I expect Bones thought I was his owner,
considering all the quality time we spent. I wished I knew

his real name. I listened sometimes, waiting under the house, but the words were usually too muffled to make out anything, unless Bob and Melodie were having a fight. Bob could get pretty loud. I went through their address book, hoping for something like *Tiger's vet,* but no clues. He answered to Lazybones— or Bones—as much as any cat answers.

I generally took a long nap each day with Bones on my chest. It was like working the night shift, except no work! I sold off a lawn mower and weed eater—garage items from down the block—and got myself a gym membership so I could shower, swim, hot tub, and work out with the hardcore sissy fellas every day if I wanted, and especially on weekends when I was stuck out of the house all day.

Things were going good. That night I was still holding some cash, and I thought I'd slug down a few shots at one of them outdoor South Beach bars, take in the fancy scenery, meaning women. It was just then, when I'd got my life all in order, I run into Boozanne. I come up to the bar and there she was, her back to me, lapping a little over the stool in the thigh area, a big girl with lots of curly orange hair and freckled white skin on her upper arms. She had on a thin nylon shirt that clung to every ripple of her, the handles of love, and the lush flesh above the back of her brassiere. When she turned my way, there were those double D's, staring at me, talcum still dry between 'em, and the smell of a baby, despite eighty-five degrees and heavy humidity. Stars were winking in the black sky over her head, so I shoulda known the joke was on me.

A flamenco guitar strummed away in my left ear, traffic and ocean crashed together in the right. "Hi, there," I yelled. I pointed at the only empty seat, the one next to her, where she had parked her pocketbook.

"I'm Junior," I said. I was more often called Mouse, but I didn't like it.

"Name's Susanne," I thought she said.

I nodded. "Pleased to meet you, Susanne."

She scrunched up her little pig nose with the freckles on it, but I didn't know what the problem was. She had a puckered set of red lips to go with that nose. "Boooz-anne," she drawled.

That there was the killer. Her voice flowed out like syrup and I damned near choked. I wondered if she could be a Kentucky girl, hot and smooth as the bourbon I'd left behind those two years ago. I musta stared at her—I wasn't sure what was polite to say.

She picked up her beer can. "Booooz-anne!" she hollered. "Buy me one."

The bartender looked at me, and I put up two fingers.

Boozanne stared at my legs. "You need a hoist onto that stool, pal?"

I ignored her and used the step under the bar to give me the extra lift. Boozanne lit a cigarette. Her cheeks sucked in and her lashes kinda flickered in pleasure as she drew the smoke. When her chin tipped back on the exhale, I remembered how ma used to aim her smoke at the ceiling by protruding her bottom lip like a funnel. Boozanne's white neck and the pattern of freckles spilling down resembled one of the girls' chests in Bob's porno video. The smoke hung in the air and the flamenco ripped to a finale as she focused on me. When she finally talked, she didn't slur.

"You're pretty cute for a shortie. Been working out?"

"Some," I said. It came to me that she might want to get

naked, and I wasn't against it.

"You know how long a man's legs are supposed to be, don't you?"

I shook my head, getting ready for a joke about my height, figuring it was worth the ridicule to get laid.

"Long enough to reach the ground," she said. "Abraham Lincoln."

"Abraham Lincoln said that?" I scratched my head. "He had real long legs, didn't he?"

"Yeah, but that's not the point. Yours are long enough."

"It all evens out horizontal, don't it?"

She laughed, and after that my memories are spotty. Sometime, Boozanne and me staggered across the street, holding hands and bumping together, and we stumbled over the sand toward the water, to my favorite wooden lounge chair, chained behind a small dune of shore grass, far enough from the street to be dark. My mind wasn't working too good, but I recall taking off my pants, falling over once.

Next thing, there was Boozanne, buck-naked and white as whip cream, like an art model with all the rich layers of her unfolding, as she laid down on the lounge and opened her arms to me. I stopped trying to brush off sand and leaned over her and straddled one of her thighs. We did some tonguing, I think, but mostly I remember the feel of her, meaty and cool, as I pawed over her big tits and nuzzled her neck. When I scooted on down, that baby powder drowned out the fishy smell of the beach. I suckled her nipples and crawled onto her lap. She weren't my first woman, but there hadn't been many, and none of this size. I poked into her soft gut and jelly thighs a few times, and then I located that sweet spot you don't never forget.

Over the next week, besides picking most of the quarters out of the change jar, I had some easy pickings from a tree service trailer, and took a chain saw to the South Dixie Pawn Shop. Boozanne—surprise, surprise—could put away the liquor, and I didn't want to seem poor. I knew I amused her, but it could all end fast if I stopped giving her what she needed. I figured I was some kind of rebound catch anyway, since otherwise she was out of my league. I convinced her to go to my usual local bar, where it was homey. Quantity was more important to her than scenery, and she didn't complain much.

Besides liking sex, she was a woman who could tell a joke. I enjoyed her stories about idiots at the office, and the quick way she saw through her boss with his snooty manners. She had some schemes for easy money, and she promised to let me in. I'd started talking to Bones about her, and when I pictured her pretty face I felt something way stronger than the tightness in my balls.

One night when we were sitting on the lounge chair smoking some weed, I dropped the roach into my shirt pocket and the damn fabric flared right up. Boozanne was fast with her hand to pat it out. "Your heart's on fire for me," she said. She was laughing, but I couldn't deny it. I took that as a sign.

Course the subject came up of going to my place instead of the sticky, sandy lounge chair, and I couldn't fend her off for long. She had an efficiency and a roommate, so it was up to me to make arrangements if I wanted to "continue enjoying her womanhood." Now, I was really working her pussy hard, and I had a suspicion that she liked the fucking as much as me, but I knew there were plenty more men where I come from—taller ones,

with better incomes—whereas she was the only woman
ever come on to me that didn't ask for money up front.
The wood chair hurt her back, and she wouldn't get on
top cause she was embarrassed about how she outweighed
me. She kept harping on it until I let loose of the truth. I
thought it would be the end of us, but it turned out my
living conditions were a real amusement. I'd lied that I was
on disability, but now I gave out all my secrets, including
my nickname Mouse—that she promised never to use—
and my recent incarceration.

Before I had time to think, she'd took the day off work,
and I was sneaking her in between the air conditioner and
Bob's garden hose. I had to bend some bushes to get her
through, and they took some damage, but probably only
Bones would notice.

I had a long sheet of plastic stretching to the edge
under the house, so I could crawl on my stomach without
getting dirty, and Boozanne surprised me with the ease
that she wormed on through. She weren't afraid of the
spiders or nothing. I went first and moved the bed aside,
and she stood and took my hand, and stepped up into the
room like a lady. It was a big hole, but she pretty much
filled it. I'd told her I could go inside and unlock the back
door for her, but she said the porch was too visible, and
that was true. She wandered around the house, while I slid
the wood to cover the hole, enough so Bones couldn't get
out, and scooted the bed back in place so the bedroom
looked nice.

Boozanne came floating my way in the living room,
with a cigarette, sipping from one of Melodie's good glasses
filled with a clear gold liquid. I only hoped it wasn't the
scotch Bob was saving from his birthday. She'd stripped off

her clothes and put on a see-through robe that left a gap in front, with pink nipples and red muff peeking out.

I grabbed her cigarette and flung it into the sink.

She clucked her tongue at me. "Such a worrier. They've got all kinds of booze in the cabinet, Junior. I'm surprised you haven't polished it off."

"Now I shoulda told you—you got to be careful. They notice things missing, and I'm out. I hope that's the Cutty's."

She tossed her curls. "Why drink Cutty's when there's Glenfiddich?"

"Okay, just take it easy. We'll add a little water. Don't open new bottles and don't drink more than a couple shots of any one thing."

"No problem. There's lots to try. I haven't had this much fun since I was twelve and broke into the neighbors'."

"Oh, yeah? What'd you do?"

"Not much. Three of us girls—we just put a little hole in the screen door and got excited sneaking around, looking in the bedrooms. Adrenaline rush."

"There is something to that," I said.

"I don't know why we didn't check for money or take anything."

"Maybe you didn't need anything."

"Oh, Junior, you always need money," she said. She cuffed me on the chest.

"I don't. Not always."

"That's why you're special—besides this."

She bent down and undid my belt and zipper, dropping my pants, and pulled me against her big powdered tits for a long sloppy kiss. I was useless, barely able to waddle over to the bed and kick my pants off my knees so I could climb on top of her. I got her breathing hard, grunting and cooing, and we were both sweating rivers. I thought for a second about messing the sheets, but I had plenty of time to run laundry.

After that Boozanne got the fancy platter out of the china cabinet, and the cloth napkins, and we ate a snack— olives and imported cheeses and crackers, a small chunk of goat cheese, Parmesan, some Stilton. I wouldn't've touched the moldy stuff on my own, but the Lamberts had introduced me to lots of new food, and most of it was pretty damn tasty. Boozanne was still hungry so I made her a peanut butter and jelly, which was always safe, but she didn't much like it.

She left around three, and I was exhausted, but there was plenty of clean up to do. I panicked when I picked up a juice glass and saw a white ring on the coffee table. I found some furniture spray that didn't work, but as I stood there pulling out my hair, the ring started to lighten up, until it finally disappeared. I did the dishes and threw the napkins into the washer with the sheets. I hoped there was no ironing required.

Bones came out from somewhere to lay on me while I waited for the fabric softener cycle. He was purring and it felt good relaxing with him on my chest after the wild afternoon. "Bones," I said, holding his head to look into his eyes. "Here's a woman who knows all about me and still likes me." I massaged behind his ears and his jaw went slack because it felt so good. "I'm pretty damned fond of her too." I couldn't say the word *love* out loud, not even to Bones.

He stared me in the face with his big gold eyes, and I thought I saw sadness. Course he always looked like that,

and just because Boozanne came around, I wasn't gonna
ditch him.

Soon Boozanne quit her job. It was understandable—
all the typing they piled on her. She was consulting with
a lawyer on some female issues. I was glad to see more
of her, but it was worrisome, her not having any money
coming in. We went on like that for a couple weeks, wild
sex and a snack several afternoons. She passed some time
looking through the Lamberts' closets and drawers. I'd
seen it all already, so I sipped whiskey and watched her
flesh move around in that skimpy robe. Lucky I had the
place memorized, cause caution was not her strong feature,
and I had to make sure everything got put back. As it was,
a wine glass got broke. She scared me sometimes, but I
couldn't think of what I used to do without her.

I picked up bottles and cans for extra money, so I
could pay for drinks at night. A couple times I did dishes
for cash. I wasn't really allowed out of Kentucky, so I
couldn't take a job that checked records. I got into a
neighbor's storage shed and found an old waffle iron and
ice skates to pawn, and let my gym membership go. There
was a workout course on the beach and I could shower
there and let my clothes dry on me Saturday and Sunday.
I didn't have much time to work out anyways with all the
hours it took to scrounge. Boozanne got some kind of
weekend job, just enough to keep up her rent, until she
could find something good. She wouldn't take no cash
from me.

In early July the Lamberts went to California for a
week. It was blocked out on their calendar for a month,
and Boozanne and me couldn't wait. Boozanne moved
right in and we took over the place. The first morning she

cooked me biscuits and fluffy eggs like her grandma taught her, and we took our time eating, and left the dishes all day, and smoked some of the weed that Boozanne found in Bob's chest of drawers. The only problem was that Bones was shipped off somewhere so we didn't have our pet. I wished I could have told Melly that I'd take care of him.

One day we were lazying around in the bedroom, and I showed Boozanne Melodie's "secret" drawer. That was a mistake. My plan was to slip one of the old rings on to her finger to see what she'd say, but she spotted Melodie's gold heart right in front. It was a real delicate necklace that was usually missing, so I knew Melodie normally wore it a lot and must have left it home for safe keeping. Boozanne became instantly attached, and I didn't want to let her take it. Necklaces can get misplaced easy, so it wasn't so much that I thought we'd get caught, but it was probably a present from Bob, or maybe even an heirloom.

Boozanne put it around her neck and asked me to fasten it. "Please, baby?" She was stroking my bicep and I liked that.

"Can you just wear it while you're here and put it back?"

"My birthday's coming up and I know you don't have money to buy me a gift."

"When's your birthday?"

"November, but you won't have any money then either."

It was true, and I had never bought her a present.

"It'll be a nice memento of our vacation," she said. "Please, baby, please?"

I suggested a small silver heart that was far back in the drawer, but she said she was allergic to any metals except gold. I felt terrible about Melodie, but seeing how pretty the gold looked in Boozanne's freckled cleavage, and how much she wanted it, I let her take it. I checked for extra Kleenexes in Melodie's bathroom trash when the Lamberts got home, and there weren't none, but deadlocks appeared on the doorjambs after the weekend, and that creeped me out. One more mistake and they'd start checking everything. I tried to get the heart back to plant it, but Boozanne wouldn't give it up. She didn't understand my feelings about the place.

Things went good for a few more weeks, and then Boozanne got tired of the job hunt and lack of money. Safe pickings for the pawn shop were running slim in the neighborhood. Boozanne said she had a plan to make some real money, live high on the hog for a while, do some traveling, then get an apartment of our own. Sneaking around was exciting at first, but she was tired of it. I didn't want to leave the Lamberts, after only two months, but my odds for getting caught were climbing, and if I wanted Boozanne, I had to go.

We were sitting on the couch, me petting Bones, when she gave me the specifics.

"I'll handle it," she said. "We've got credit cards, social security numbers, birth certificates, check books, bank statements, passports, and salable goods. You've heard of identity theft."

"But they're nice people. Melodie is. I don't want to steal from them."

"What are you talking about? You've been stealing from them for months."

"Not enough to matter."

"That's what I'm saying. It's time to do something that

matters. They've got almost $10,000 in their checking account."

"I can't," I said. "They're like relatives."

"And I'm not?"

When she put it like that, I had no argument. I'd only seen them at a distance and in pictures, but it still didn't feel right.

"You don't have to do anything," she said. She went to the desk and brought back some insurance papers. "Look, they're well-insured for their possessions—and the credit cards pay for fraudulent charges. I won't write checks if you don't want me to. It seems tricky anyway."

"I can cut a hole somewhere else for the burglaring."

"Too much trouble and you might not be as lucky. Besides, I already started." She pulled two credit cards out of her pocketbook and held them in front of my face. There was one card for Melodie and one for Robert.

It was all real then, and my guts were shot out. "Jesus," I said.

"We've got their other cards, plus these new ones I applied for, $5,000 limit on each."

She dug back into her pocketbook and pulled out a small satin pouch. I looked inside and saw the glitter of gold and cut stones. "Necklace and earring set—off the internet. I've got more stuff coming. We can get cash for these, and I bet you can find somebody to buy the passports."

It was too late to stop her without calling in the law.

She patted my head. "I'll get us flights to anywhere you want. You deserve it, baby."

I let her kiss me then, and my mind went into a haze, a kind of protective vision of us sipping bourbon on the

porch swing of some cozy cottage in the mountains of
Kentucky, Boozanne exhaling smoke into a cool summer
breeze.

Three weeks later was moving day. Boozanne had
bought two suitcases on wheels, filled them with our new
clothes and more high-end jewelry pieces she'd ordered.
She was busy wrapping up old silver trays she'd found in
a chest. I'd liquidated the necklace and earrings and some
nice watches, and we had $6,000 cash, airline tickets and
room reservations for someplace exotic—a surprise—
and the new credit cards to charge whatever we needed
when we got there. Visa and Master Charge had called
about unusual activity, but Boozanne answered all their
questions. We took the bills for those old cards out of the
mailbox, so we had plenty of leeway. She figured we could
vacation for two weeks and still have resources to rent
a place when we got back. When we ran low on money,
we'd start over again. I was excited about traveling with
Boozanne, but I hated ripping off the Lamberts. They'd
been good to me, in their way.

I'd finished wiping all the furniture and appliances
for fingerprints and closed the suitcases, and Boozanne
was wearing rubber gloves, still poking around. Bones
was sleeping on the couch, and I gave him a goodbye pet,
feeling real sad.

I went into the kitchen and looked at the clock. I
couldn't believe it. "Damn!" I yelled. "It's a quarter to
seven!"

I went back into the living room. She was searching the
bottom drawers of the desk.

"Boozanne! We gotta go. It's not like we're headed to a
movie."

"Five minutes. I don't want to miss anything. Money goes fast on vacation."

"We're cutting it too close. I never stay this late."

"No worries." Just then she opened the drawer with the folders of silver dollars. I held my breath, hoping she'd pass them by again, thinking they were books.

She flipped open the first cover. "Oh, wow!" She lifted them out and carried them to the coffee table. She opened another and another.

"We don't have room for those old coins. They're too heavy," I told her.

She pulled out a dollar and studied it. "Mouse, these could be worth a fortune! They're antique silver dollars."

"Naw, put 'em down. You're allergic to silver. We gotta get out of here."

"No, way. Open the suitcase."

"Boozanne, I won't take 'em. They're Melodie's inheritance. It's all she got."

"You're insane. You with your freaky crush. Now open that suitcase, or I will. I'll leave you here with your fucking Melodie."

I didn't have time to let that sink in. There was the sound of a car pulling into the carport. "Jesus Christ," I whispered. I ducked and took a glance out the corner of the window. "It's her." I grabbed Boozanne's hand, but she didn't budge. "Come on!" I hollered. We can make it out the hole."

"I'm not leaving without the coins."

I just stood there, unable to gather a thought. She was digging into her pocketbook.

"Stand next to the door," she said. "Grab her mouth from behind and hold her."

I did what I was told, and Boozanne ducked around
the corner. In seconds, the key turned and poor Melly
stepped inside. I yanked her from behind, clamping a
hand over her mouth and kicking the door shut before she
could scream. I pulled her down against me and fell half
on top of her. She was more delicate than I thought, and
her face had wrinkles I couldn't see in the pictures, but she
was beautiful. My eyes filled because I knew I hurt her.
She whimpered and my heart broke. When I looked up,
Boozanne was bent over, those double D's loose near my
head, her shirt pulled up covering her face and hair. It was
nylon, and she was stretching it so she could see through
the thin mesh. A .25 in her other hand pointed straight
into Melodie's ear.

"What the fuck?" I was so stunned I let go of Melodie's
mouth and she screamed and yanked her face sideways. I
cut her off fast, and pushed her head under my armpit, but
she'd already seen my face. Bones was there staring at me,
his eyes huge, not knowing whose side to be on.

"Move aside!" yelled Boozanne.

All I could think of was sweet Melodie's brains
splattered on my shirt. I grabbed the barrel of the gun and
tilted it toward the ceiling. "Go!" I yelled. "You go! I'll hold
her while you get away."

"You sure?" she said. She didn't sound too
disappointed.

"Hurry up."

She blew me a kiss, opened a suitcase, threw out my
clothes, and dropped in the books of coins. I stayed on top
of Melodie, my head sagging onto her neck. I could smell
her hair, clean and flowery. I tried to soothe her by stroking
it. Bones gave paw onto my cheek, but seeing no treats,

climbed up and laid on my back. I watched the squeaky wheels of the suitcases roll past my nose.

"We could've been great together," she said, "if one of us was a different person."

I looked up and thought I saw a glint of tears in her eye, as she shut the door. Boozanne was gone, taking my dreams with her.

It all hit me then—Melodie had no idea I'd saved her life, and she was never gonna think of me like a brother. She'd freak when she found out how long I'd been living there, even if I did keep the house nice and feed Bones. Some of her ribs were likely broken. I'd never be able to explain. I was headed back to the slammer for a long, long time.

I thought about Boozanne. I didn't even know her real name and hadn't never seen those airplane tickets to ponder where she was headed. It could've been so perfect, if she hadn't got greedy. Our plan was to walk down to the bar, have a beer, call a taxi to the airport. . . . She wouldn't do that now.

Bob's car pulled in, and I was still laying there, half on Melodie. My arm went limp, and Bones jumped off my back as I sat up. Melly rolled to her side wailing, her eyes flat as those silver dollars. I said, "Sorry, so sorry, Mel," but she didn't hear.

I leaned against the wall and pictured Boozanne, down the block, big and bold as she was, sticking out her thumb—and a gold Cadillac stopping, its doors opening up like wings, to fly her away.

ReBecca

As her Siamese twin joined at the skull, I know Becca
wants to fuck Remus as soon as she says she's going to dye
our hair. I don't say anything — yet. I'm not sure she's even
admitting it to herself. The idea doesn't sit well with me,
but I decide to wait and see just how she plans to go about
it.

It's a warm, clear night, a breeze rattling the palms,
a nice walk to Walgreen's, although we hobble. Becca
picks out a light magenta hair-color that to me suggests
heavy drug addiction. "No, siree," I tell her. "I know my
complexion colors. I'm a fall, and that's definitely a spring."
No spring that ever existed in nature, I might add.

"Oh, stop it, Rebby. We'll do a middle part and you can
keep your flat brown and I'll just liven up my side. I want
to get it shaped too — something that falls around my
face."

"It better not fall anywhere near my face."

When we get home from the drugstore, she reads the
instructions aloud and there are about fifty steps to this
process by the time you do the lightening and the toning.
Then she starts telling me which hairs are hers and which
are mine. We've gone around on this before. It's a tough
problem because our faces aren't set exactly even: I look

left and down while she faces straight ahead and up. For
walking we've managed a workable system where I watch
for curbs and ground objects and she spots branches
and low-flying aircraft. She claims to have saved our life
numerous times.

"Oh, yeah? And for what?" I always ask her. And
she laughs. But now I know — so she can fuck Remus,
the pale scrawny clerk with the goatee who works at A
Different Fish down the corner. Now it's clear why Becca
didn't laugh when I pointed out his resemblance to the
suckermouth catfish. Also her sudden decision to raise
crayfish. Those bastards are mean, ugly sons of bitches, but
they suit Becca just fine. They're always climbing out of the
tank to dehydrate under the couch, so we have to go back
to the store for new ones. Fuck — I'd rather die a virgin.
We entertain ourself just fine.

It's two A.M. when she finishes drying that magenta
haystack and we finally get into bed. Then she stays awake
mooning about Remus while I put a beanbag lizard over
my eyes and try to turn off her side of the brain. I know
where she's got her fingers. There's a tingle and that certain
haziness in our head.

We barely make it to work on time in the morning.
Then Becca talks one of our coworkers into giving her a
haircut during lunch. The woman is a beautician, but she
developed allergies to the chemicals, so now she works at
the hospital lab with us.

They're snipping and flipping hair in the break-room to
beat shit while I'm trying to eat my tuna fish. "Yes!" Becca
says, when she looks in the mirror. Her side is blunt-cut
into a sort of swinging pageboy. She tweaks the wave over
her eye, making sure we'll be clobbered by a branch in the

near future.

We get home from work that evening and — surprise — she counts the crayfish and reports another missing. I try to scramble down to look under the couch in case the thing hasn't dried out yet, but she braces her legs and I can't get the leverage.

"You know how much trouble it is for us to get back up," she says. "Anyway, it'd be covered with dust-bunnies and hair."

At that moment I get a flash of guilt from her section of the brain — she's lying. There is no fucking arthropod under the couch. She wants badly to get back into that aquarium store.

I catch Becca smiling sweetly at me in the hall mirror. I forgive her.

She insists on changing into "sleisure wear" — that's what I call it — to walk down the street. The frock's a short fresh pink number with cut-in shoulders. I'm wearing my "Dead Babies" tour T-shirt and the cutoffs I wore all last weekend. Becca has long given up trying to get me to dress in tandem.

We see Remus through the glass door when we get there. He has his back to us dipping out feeders for a customer. His shaved white neck almost glows. The little bell rings as we step in. Becca tugs me toward the tank where the crayfish are, and I can tell she's nervous.

Remus turns. Straining my peripheral vision, I catch the smile he throws her. I can feel this mutual energy between them that I missed before. He's not too bad-looking with a smile. I start to imagine what it's going to be like. What kind of posture they'll get me into. Maybe I should buy earplugs and a blindfold.

Becca heads toward the crayfish, but I halt in front of a saltwater tank of neon-bright fish and corals. A goby pops its round pearly head out of a mounded hole in the sandy bottom and stares at us. "Look," I say, "he's like a little bald-headed man," but she just keeps trudging on to the crayfish tank, where she pretends to look for a healthy specimen. Remus comes back with his dipper and a plastic bag.

"What can I do for you two lovely ladies tonight?"

Becca blushes and giggles. Remus reddens. I know he's thinking about his use of the number two. He's got it right, but he's self-conscious . . . like everybody.

She points to the largest, meanest-looking crawdad in sight. "This guy," she says. I figure she's after the upper-body strength, the easier he can knock the plastic lid off our tank and boost himself out over the edge. "Think you can snag him?" she asks Remus.

He takes it as a test. "You bet. Anything for my best customer — s." He stands on tiptoe so the metal edge of the tank is in his armpit and some dark hair curls from his scrunched short sleeve. He dunks the sleeve completely as he swoops and chases that devil around the corners of the tank.

Remus is no fool. He's noticed Becca's new haircut and color. I'm thinking, get your mind outta the gutter, buster — but I'm softening. I'm tuned to Becca's feelings, and I'm curious about this thing — although, it's frightening. Not so much the sex, but the idea of three. I'm used to an evenly divided opinion, positive and negative, side by side, give and take. We might be strange to the world, but we've developed an effective system. Even his skinny bones on her side of the balance could throw it all off.

Remus catches the renegade and flips him into the

plastic bag, filling it halfway with water. He pulls a twist-tie from his pocket and secures the bag. "You have plenty of food and everything?" Remus asks.

Becca nods slowly and pokes at the bag. I know she's trying to think of a way to start something without seeming too forward. Remus looks like he's fishing for a thought.

My portion of the gray matter takes the lead. "Hey," I say, "Becca and I were thinking we'd try a new brownie recipe and rent a video. Wanna stop by on your way home?"

Becca twitches. I feel a thrill run through her, then apprehension. She turns our head further to Remus. "Want to?" she says.

"Sure. I don't get out of here till nine. Is that too late?"

"That's fine," I say. I feel her excitement as she gives him the directions to the house and we head out.

When we get outside she shoots into instant panic. "What brownie recipe? We don't even have flour!"

"Calm down," I tell her. "All he's thinking about is that brownie between your legs."

"Geez, Reb, you're so crude."

"Chances are he won't even remember what we invited him for." Suddenly, it hits me that he could be thinking about what's between my legs too — a natural ménage à trois. I rethink — no way, Remus wouldn't know what to do with it.

Becca insists that we make brownies. She pulls me double-time the three blocks to the Seven-Eleven to pick up a box mix. I grab a pack of M&M's and a bag of nuts. "Look, we'll throw these in and it'll be a new recipe."

She brightens and nods our head. I can feel her warmth

rush into me because she knows I'm on her side — in more ways than one, for a change.

We circle the block to hit the video store in the strip mall and Becca agrees to rent *What Ever Happened to Baby Jane?* She hates it, but it's my favorite, and she's not in the mood to care. I pick it off the shelf and do my best Southern Bette Davis: "But, Blanche, you are in that wheelchair."

It's eight o'clock when we get home and the first thing Becca wants to do is hop in the shower. I'd rather start the brownies. We both make a move in opposite directions, like when we were little girls. She fastens onto the loveseat and I get a grip on the closet doorknob. Neither of us is going anywhere.

"Reb, please, let go!" she hollers.

After a few seconds of growling, I realize we're having a case of nerves. I let go and race Becca into the bathroom. "Thanks, Rebelle," she says.

At 9:10 we slide the brownies into the oven and hear a knock. Remus made good time. I notice Becca's quick intake of breath and a zinging in our brain.

Remus has a smile that covers his whole face. I feel Becca's cheek pushing my scalp and can figure a big grin on her too. I hold back my wiseass grumbling. So this is love.

Becca asks Remus in and we get him a Bud. He's perched on the loveseat. Our only choice is the couch, which puts me between them, so I slump into my "invisible" posture, chin on chest, and suck my beer. I know that way Becca is looking at him straight on.

"The brownies will be ready in a little while. Want to see the movie?" she asks.

"Sure."

Becca tries to stand, but I'm slow to respond.

Remus jumps up and heads for the VCR. "Let me," he says.

"Relax," I whisper to Becca. I'm thinking, thank God I've got Baby Jane for amusement.

The movie comes on and neither of them speaks. Maybe the video wasn't such a good idea. I start spouting dialogue just ahead of Bette whenever there's a pause. Becca shushes me.

The oven timer goes off. "The brownies," I say. "We'll be right back." We hustle into the kitchen and I get them out. Becca tests them with the knife in the middle. "Okay," I tell her, "I'm going to get you laid."

"Shh, Reb!" I feel her consternation, but she doesn't object.

The brownies are too hot to cut, so Becca picks up the pan with the hot pad and I grab dessert plates, napkins and the knife. "Just keep his balls out of my face," I say.

That takes the wind out of her, but I charge for the living room.

Remus has moved to the right end of the couch. Hmm. My respect for him is growing.

We watch and eat. Remus comments on how good the brownies are. Becca giggles and fidgets. Remus offers to get us another beer from the fridge. Becca says no thanks. He brings me one.

"Ever had a beer milkshake?" I ask him.

"Nope."

"How 'bout a Siamese twin?"

His mouth falls open and I'm thinking suckermouth catfish all the way, but his eyes have taken on focus.

I tilt my face up. "Becca would shoot me for saying this

— if she could do it and survive — but I know why you're
here, and I know she finds you attractive, so I don't see a
reason to waste any more time."

The silence is heavy and all of a sudden the TV blares
— "You wouldn't talk to me like that if I wasn't in this
chair —" "But, Blanche, you are in that chair, you are in
that chair."

"Shut that off," I tell Remus.

He breaks from his paralysis and does it.

I feel Becca's face tightening into a knot, but there are
sparks behind it.

I suggest moving into the bedroom where it's cooler.
Remus gawks.

I'm named Rebelle so Mom could call both of us at
once — she got a kick out of her cleverness — and I take
pride in being rebellious. I drag Becca up.

She's got the posture of a hound dog on a leash, but her
secret thrill runs down my backbone. I think our bodies
work like the phantom-limb sensation of amputees. We
get impulses from the brain, even when our own physical
parts aren't directly stimulated. I'm determined to do what
her body wants and not give her mind a chance to stop it.
She follows along. We get into the bedroom and I set us
down. Remus sits next to Becca. Without a word, he bends
forward and kisses her, puts his arms around her and
between our bodies. I watch.

It's an intense feeling, waves of heat rushing over me,
heading down to my crotch. We've been kissed before, but
not like this. He works at her mouth and his tongue goes
inside.

The kissing stops. Remus looks at me, then turns
back to Becca. He takes her face in his hands and puts his

lips on her neck. I can smell him and hear soft kisses. My
breathing speeds up. Becca starts to gasp.

He stops and I hear the zipper on the back of her dress.
She stiffens, but he takes her face to his again and we slide
back into warm fuzzies. This Remus has some style. He
pulls the dress down to her waist and unhooks her bra. She
shrugs it off.

"You're beautiful," he tells her.

"Thanks," I say. I get a jolt of Becca's annoyance.

My eyes are about a foot from her nipples, which are
up like gobies, and he gets his face right down in them,
takes the shining pink nubs into his mouth and suckles. I
feel myself edging toward the warm moist touch of his lips,
but the movement is mostly in my mind.

Remus pushes Becca onto the pillow and I fall along
and lie there, my arms to my side. He lifts her hips and
slides the dress down and off, exposing a pair of white lace
panties that I never knew Becca had, never even saw her
put on.

He nuzzles the perfect V between her legs and licks
those thighs, pale as cave fish. Becca reaches up and starts
unbuttoning his shirt. He helps her, then speedily slips his
jeans down to the floor, taking his underwear with them. I
stare. This is first time we've seen one live. I feel a tinge of
fear and I don't know if it's from Becca or me.

"Got a condom?" I ask him.

"Oh, yeah," he says. He reaches for his pants and pulls
a round gold package out of the pocket. Becca puts her
hand on my arm while he's opening it, and I turn my chin
to her side and kiss her shoulder. We both watch while he
places the condom flat on the tip of his penis and slowly
smoothes it down.

He gets to his knees, strips off the lace panties and puts his mouth straight on her. His tongue works in and I can feel the juices seeping out of me in response. Becca starts cooing like those cockatiels we used to have, and I bite my lip not to make a noise. Remus moves up and guides himself in, and I swear I can feel the stretching and burning. I'm clutching my vaginal muscles rigid against nothing, but it's the fullest, most intense feeling I've ever had.

Becca starts with sound effects from *The Exorcist*, and I join right in because I know she can't hear me over her own voice, and Remus is puffing and grunting enough not to give a fuck about anything but the fucking. His hip bumps mine in fast rhythm, as the two of them locked together pound the bed. I clench and rock my pelvis skyward and groan with the need, stretching tighter and harder, until I feel a letting-down as if an eternal dam has broken. I'm flooded with a current that lays me into the mattress and brings out a long, thready weep. It's like the eerie love song of a sperm whale. I sink into the blue and listen to my breathing and theirs settle down.

I wake up later and look to my side. Remus has curled next to Becca with one arm over her chest and a lock of the magenta hair spread across his forehead. His fingers are touching my ribs through my shirt, but I know he doesn't realize it. I have tears in my eyes. I want to be closer, held tight in the little world of his arms, protected, loved — but I know he is hers now, and she is his. I'm an invisible attachment of nerves, muscles, organs and bones.

It's after one when we walk Remus to the door, and he tells Becca he'll call her at work the next day. He gives her a long, gentle kiss, and I feel her melting into sweet cream inside.

"Good night — I mean good morning," Remus says to me. He gives me a salute. Comrades, it means. It's not a feeling I can return, but I salute back. I know he sees the worry in my eyes. I try to take my mind out of the funk, before Becca gets a twinge.

Remus calls her twice that afternoon, and a pattern takes shape over the next three days: whispered calls at work, a walk down the street after dinner, a 9:10 Remus visitation. I act gruff and uninterested.

When we go to bed I try not to get involved. You'd think once I'd seen it, I could block it out, catch up on some sleep. But the caresses are turning more sure and more tender, the sounds more varied — delicate but strong with passion, unearthly. My heart is cut in two — like Becca and I should be. I'm happy for her, but I'm miserably lonely.

On the third day, I can't hold back my feelings anymore. Of course, Becca knows already. It's time to compromise.

"I think we should limit Remus's visits to twice a week. I'm tired everyday at work and I can't take this routine every night. Besides," I tell her, "you shouldn't get too serious. This can't last."

Becca sighs with relief. "I thought you were going to ask me to share."

I don't say anything. It had crossed my mind.

"Just give us a few more nights," she says. "He's bound to need sleep sometime too." I notice her use of the pronoun *us*, that it doesn't refer to Becca and me anymore.

She puts her arm around my shoulder and squeezes. "I know it's hard, but —"

"Seems to me that's your only interest — how hard it is."

I feel the heat of her anger spread across into my scalp. I've hit a nerve. She's like a stranger.

"You can't undermine this, Reb. It's my dream."

"We've been taking care of each other all our lives. Now you're treating me like a tumor. What am I supposed to do?"

"What can I do? It's not fair!" she screams. Her body is shaking.

"It's not my fault, for Christ's sake!" I turn toward her, which makes her head turn away. She starts to sob.

I take my hand to her far cheek. I wipe the tears. I can't cause her more pain.

"I'm sorry. I know I'm cynical and obnoxious. But if I don't have a right to be, who does?" I stop for a second. "Well I guess you do . . . So how come you're not?"

"Nobody could stand us," she sniffs.

I smooth her hair till she stops crying. "I love you, Becca . . . Fuck — I'll get earplugs and a blindfold."

That night we take our walk down the street. There's nobody in the store but Remus. He walks up and I feel Becca radiating pleasure just on sight. He gives her a peck on the cheek.

I smell his scent. I'm accustomed to it. I try to act cheerful. I've pledged to let this thing happen, but I can almost feel him inside of her already, and the overwhelming gloom that follows. I put a finger in my ear and start humming "You Can't Always Get What You Want" to block them out. Then it hits me.

"Headphones — that's what I need. I can immerse myself in music."

"What?" asks Remus.

"Oh, nothing," I say, and then whisper to Becca, "I've found a solution." I give her a hug. I'll work with her, even on this.

The little bell on the door rings. Remus turns to see behind us. "Hey there, Rom," he calls, "how was the cichlid convention?" He looks back at us. "Did I mention my brother? He's just home from L.A."

Becca and I turn and do a double double-take. In the last dusky rays of sunset stands a mirror image of Remus — identical, but a tad more attractive. A zing runs through my brain. I know Becca feels it, too.

Must Bite!

I thought I'd seen everything and survived it—and I was fucking sick of it. I'd been dancing in Key Largo for four years, since age twenty-one, and men were nothing but work to me. I enjoyed women's company better—but since women were a dead end economically, I was looking for a dick with major dollar signs flashing. I was ready to pack up for Miami because summer in the Keys was such poor pickings. Then came my lucky night, the night Rex turned up.

Sleaze, the manager, came into the club dressing room to get me, so I knew he'd got a tip.

"He wants the monkey," Sleaze told me. "That be you."

"The monkey?" I caught my breath. "Who is he?" Spunky Monkey was the nickname Pop gave me back home in Indiana, but he was long dead, and nobody in the Keys knew the name.

"Guy in his 40's. Big guy. Wad of cash."

"He asked for Monkey?"

"Yeah. You used the trapeze last number, right?"

I nodded.

Sleaze jerked his thumb toward the bar.

"Cool." I tossed on a robe over my bare shoulders and moved my ass out. I had a real acrobatics performance and I felt appreciated when it wasn't wasted on a bunch of drooly burnouts. The usual crowd didn't care if you could keep time with the music, as long as they could smell your cunt. Tips were lean at Reefers, and a special request meant I could set my own price, the best kind of reward.

I was compact and muscular, and kept up my gymnast skills from junior high. Being called Monkey was a compliment, although, as a redhead, I had less body hair than most of the girls. With big blue eyes, I didn't really look like a monkey.

Rex was facing toward me from the bar, catching my titty action as I walked, what little there was. Attractive, considering he was close to fifty. Had a tan face, salt and pepper hair, and a hard, smooth jaw. About twice my size, sitting down. I was barely a hundred pounds, the smallest chick during off-season. I took my stance in front of him, legs wide, hands on hips, robe thrown back on my arms. It was how I met all the big boys.

"I'm Darlene. Lap dance?"

"Let me look and decide."

He'd seen all there was, since I'd already swung naked with my legs wide open, a foot over his head. But I turned around and bent over, lifting the robe to my waist. The thin chain of the G-string didn't cover my little shaved mound from behind, and I got wet, feeling his eyes hone in.

Pop always told me it was a good thing to enjoy your work because that's mostly what life is made of. Too bad I didn't enjoy it quite enough.

I bent farther and looked between my legs. His mouth was half open, and I got a sudden need for his tongue, like I could come the instant it split me.

"I'd like a date," he said.

I stood up and turned around. "I don't do dates." I always lied to get the price up.

"Never?"

"Not much."

He grabbed my arm as I started to walk away and showed me three hundreds. I asked for four. His place. After work. He'd wait outside.

When I came out a little after two, it was raining and smelled like a jungle, musty and thick, mosquitoes swarming the light under the awning, waiting to bite, tree frogs with their creepy grunts. There was one car, sparkling under the low streaming palms, headlights shining through the downpour, beacons to my fate. He pulled up, and the passenger side opened. I slung my ass on the leather seat. "Cool Mercedes."

He smiled at my thin wet shirt and held out his hand for me to shake. "Rex."

He turned left behind Shell World, and we passed Blue Fin Marina, then snaked down a long private drive. It was dark. Dripping vines and fronds dragged across my window, and the Mercedes bumped along slow. He pulled under a concrete block, two-story stilt house, and when I got out I could hear the lapping of water out back and caught the scent of rotten eggs that reminds you when it's low tide in the Keys.

He motioned me up the stairs on the side and flicked on a light. We passed sacks of feed and huge empty cages, scratched mirrors, a rope ladder, chewed-up rubber toys, and a large doll, her eyes following me. Rex crooked his finger in my direction, and I climbed the stairs, wondering if I'd get a chance to see what this was all about. He seemed to have a rule about not talking. I could handle it.

Rex opened the door to a Florida room with a built-in bar, lots of shiny bottles on the shelves, sparkling mirror tiles. He picked up a glass. I shook my head. I'd had too much of that sickening champagne at the club. He put his finger to his lips, and I followed him past two closed doors with small barred windows, tiptoeing. Sounds of huffing, snoring, and heavy movement came from inside. Must be renting out rooms to crazy old farts, I thought. He led me upstairs to the loft. The rain had stopped, and clouds drifted over the moon outside the balcony window.

Rex wasn't the usual trick. He didn't act cool or order me around. He took me in his arms and kissed my neck, breathing hot, and held back my hair to uncover more skin. Normally, I would have broken it off and set some rules, but I was geared up to think that something interesting could come of this, with all his bucks. I dropped my snotty whore act and let myself go. He held my head back and planted the softest kisses on my mouth. His breath was sweet, no garlic, no rotten teeth, no cigarettes. I wondered how he was with mine. I kissed him back and he had to cut it off to get a breath.

He stripped me down so softly, I felt like I was the one who paid. I held onto the dresser as he knelt in front of me, his fingers opening me up for his tongue. I felt myself melting, legs going weak. He pulled me on top of him and slipped in his hard cock, smooth and wide.

I let him do everything he wanted, not for the money, but because it felt so good, slow hip-slapping, deep penetration, me on top, his fingers pulling at my cheeks. I let my world dissolve. I was loose as a rag doll, but he held me close and kept me moving, until I came from his cock, something that didn't happen very often. In all the years since Pop turned me out, I'd never felt so appreciated by a man.

That night he made sure I'd want to see more of him. He knew how good he was, and the attention I needed. I'm sure he'd searched for a girl like me in all the local places, my athletic build and helpful personality, my need to get out of that disgusting club. And a nickname like Monkey. When I told him how he hit on that, I saw the light come into his eyes. I was a perfect fit.

The next morning I opened my eyes to bright sun sneaking through the blinds. I was surprised at the clean tropical style of the bedroom. No sign of mismatched furniture with broken arms or rings from glasses, no scary stained sheets, not even a scratchy couch with burn holes, like most Key Largo guys seemed to own. The bed and nightstands were heavy-duty bamboo, stuff I'd buy if I saw it in a thrift shop. He had orchids and other plants outside on the balcony.

"Nice place," I said when I saw his eyes open.

"Want to stay?"

I tried to calculate a price for the day.

"Come on. Let me show you around."

I started to climb out of bed, but my foot got tangled in the sheet and he caught me before I fell. His hands went straight to my hips. I couldn't resist that tongue. He dug right in, and it was an hour before we dragged ourselves out.

"Now you stand behind me when I open the door," he said. We were outside of one of the two doors on the first floor. I stepped back so I could only see his big body. "Hey, guys," he called out. "I have somebody for you to meet." He turned to me. "It's okay. They're relaxed."

He stepped aside. I knew these were not going to be humans from the sounds I could hear. There they were, four monkeys, two of them nearly my size, looking at me. The smallest one had a finger in its mouth, like a child. The ceiling was high, must've been two-stories, and there were trapezes mounted on beams. The windows were barred. A few piles of shit were off to the sides, and one wall had a hole punched through the plasterboard, exposing more bars inside the wall. I could see through a barred door in the middle of the wall that there was a bigger monkey in the next room.

"Hear No Evil, Think No Evil, and Speak No Evil?" I asked, pointing one, two, three. "I'm not sure of the order."

"They're not quite that well-behaved."

Two of them came over and I reached down to take the hand held out to me. The long fingers were warm and light, like a sweet pair of leather gloves.

Rex touched their heads gently. "These are spider monkeys, females, Itsy and Bitsy."

"Went up the waterspout?"

"You got it, but don't give me credit for those names, either. The other two are Mack and Sweetums, male and female."

I could see what seemed to be penises hanging from three of their asses, but no balls. "*Females?*"

"Spider monkeys have elongated vaginas. It makes mating impossible, except when they're fertile, every four years. Rape-proofing."

"The boys must get horny."

"Mack masturbates often—although not as much as Big Man." He pointed into the next room.

Sweetums stayed back, but Mack came up and took my

hand, putting my fingers into the coarse hair on his back.
I started to scratch and he leaned into it. "Don't let him
get carried away," said Rex. I took my hand off, and sure
enough Mack grabbed my wrist and forced my hand back
between his shoulder blades.

"They're willful." Rex pried the long fingers from my
wrist and disentangled the legs and tail clutching my
thigh. He took Mack's wrists in one hand and pushed his
body back with his shoulder. Mack arched and squirmed,
making shrill shrieks. Rex tossed him into the mattress in
the corner.

"Dash!"

I broke for the door and Rex pushed it almost closed
behind us, but not quite, because he had to stop and tuck a
small hand inside. "They like you," he said. "A lot. I knew it.
Be careful what you start."

"Don't they usually like people?"

"Not really."

"So where did you get all these monkeys?" I could hear
the other one rumbling around, wanting attention.

He locked the door, and opened the next room.
A monkey was waiting for us and took my hand in his
warm grip. "This is the chimp, Big Man. He's an ape, not a
monkey. He was named when I got him. You'll see why."

"I do already," I said. "He's as tall as me."

"That's not what I mean." He used his fingers to sign
words as he spoke to Big Man. "Darlene-friend," he said.
Big Man puckered up his lips, but I couldn't quite bring
myself to kiss him.

Rex took my hand and motioned me to walk out in
front of him. Big Man glared but didn't move. Rex turned
and signed. "Bye, bye. Breakfast time." He shut the door

and locked it.

"You taught them sign language?"

"No, when we bought Big Man they told us he knew signs. I learned some words so I could talk to him, but he never talks back. I think he understands though."

"What about the spiders?"

"They don't pay much attention."

"Big Man must be bored."

"I entertain him. One chimp is hard enough to handle. Come on. I'll get their breakfast."

Rex led me into the kitchen. It was huge, with two stainless steel refrigerators. He opened one filled with vegetables. "I knew they'd take to you."

"I like them too," I said.

I was starving, but I didn't say anything because the animals were waiting. They were hungry and dependent on Rex, and it was my fault that breakfast was late. I insisted on helping. We set everything out on the long preparation table and sink. I washed pounds of carrots, celery, and bags of apples, while Rex rinsed heads of lettuce. We divided the vegetables onto two trays and poured the monkey chow into the five bowls with their names.

Together we served them, first Big Man, then Itsy and Bitsy, Sweetums and Mack. I stood outside the window and watched them eat. Big Man sat and stuffed his face with a head of lettuce, pieces falling from his open mouth, making a big wet mess on the floor as he chewed, showing us how starved he was because we stayed upstairs fucking. Itsy and Bitsy chowed down too, occasionally glancing over their shoulders at me. I knew the feeling, your meals being in someone else's control. Been there.

Rex sponged up the water and dirt we'd left on the

counter top, while I made the coffee.

"So where did you get them?" I asked him.

"It was a business."

"Monkey business?"

He laughed. "You got it."

"Circus?"

"No, a petting zoo of sorts, with some shows. The stage and big cages are still outside. It was my ex's idea, Julia. She taught them the tricks and it was fun—for a while. We never made money, spent it all on food and vet care, but she had money anyway. 'The Monkey Hut' was her hobby. You want some bacon and eggs?"

"Sure. And then she split?"

"She left me the place and investments so I could take care of the monkeys."

"Ouch," I said.

"She was generous. It was my fault. We never talked."

"She never complained?"

"She might've."

He put a skillet on the stove and went to the second refrigerator and pulled out a package of bacon and a carton of eggs. "They'll smell this," he said. "Ignore the noise. I don't give them meat. Spider monkeys are vegetarian, and Big Man gets too wild. He wants it all."

The bacon had barely started to sizzle, when there was a loud howl. Others took up the scream and then there was pounding, like one was beating a tray. The screeching got louder and one of them started banging on the door.

"Metal doors?" I asked.

"Yeah, don't worry. They'll settle down in a minute."

It took about five minutes, but I thought, fuck, Rex is a kind man to care for all these animals, and I could live in a

place like this. He could even make me come, unusual for a
man. By then I didn't have any romantic notions. I'd settle
for a nice home, some monkeys to play with. I was sure I
could still get out now and then with my girlfriends. So
Rex was devoted to monkeys, and I was the new monkey.
That must have flickered in his mind when he saw me, and
I had nothing against it—if enough money came my way.

Over the next month, Rex picked me up almost every
night. I got on well with everybody. Rex and I took care of
their meals together, and I scratched backs and gave treats.
"The kids" brightened up every time I came into their
rooms. At dusk, I fixed the strawberry yogurt, oatmeal, and
flan combination that filled out their dietary needs. They'd
stick their little faces into it or squeeze it through their
fingers and lick it off. I felt appreciated, more than I'd ever
have expected, more than most of my life.

I told Rex if he installed a big trapeze in the spiders'
room, I could swing with them. He had it up in two days,
no surprise. I climbed up naked and went into my act,
swinging with my ass on the bar, then dropping to hang by
my knees. But before I got any farther, Mack swung over
and whipped past me, switching from hands to feet to tail
and flinging himself to the other trapezes and back again.
I couldn't compete. He scared me, coming so close, but
he was perfect in his moves. Sweetums joined in and soon
they were both swinging fast and switching hands, feet,
and tails, synchronizing with each other. I pulled myself up
to watch.

"Don't stop," Rex hollered. "I want to see you, not
them."

I hung by my arms and swung a little. I pulled my legs
above my body in a split across the bar, like I'd done the

first night he saw me.

He came over and gave me a greedy stare. The trapeze was just high enough for him to reach my vital parts, no accident, and he slurped at me a couple of times as I swung toward him, and then he grabbed. The monkeys kept cavorting around us, but he ate me like a starving man, ignoring them, and I hung limp on the trapeze, all feeling concentrated in one spot. When I opened my eyes, all four spiders were watching, and Big Man was staring from the next room and grunting.

I wasn't sure who thought of marriage first, but things moved fast. A captain friend of Rex's married us on his sailboat, and we put on a party at Reefers. Sleaze got in some decent champagne specially for me. I was glad to be saying goodbye to that place, and all the sucking-up that went with it.

We'd planned on a honeymoon in the Bahamas for a few days, but on the morning after the wedding, Bitsy got sick, and we had to cancel. Rex was afraid to leave her with the sitter, a teenage boy that was supposed to stop by. She didn't look that sick to me, no puking or diarrhea, but she just stayed on the mattress and held her stomach instead of eating her breakfast. Rex said that was a sure sign. When we'd cancelled our flight and looked in on her, she'd gotten up and was eating the remains from Itsy. I thought sure she'd faked her illness, but it was too late to worry about it. Rex promised we could try again soon, but the kids didn't like just anybody, and they needed lots of human interaction everyday. It wasn't any big deal. The monkeys were more fun than most people I knew.

I had them spoiled in the first week. I started giving them an extra treat or two each day, a cookie or a few crackers. They loved French fries too, but I was careful not to go too far with the grease. None of them would keep a diaper on. I hadn't counted on so much shit. It seemed to pile up more and more, maybe from the treats, or else Rex was falling down on the cleaning. I hadn't bargained on it, but I started pitching in on shit detail. They were mine now, too, and they would cuddle and kiss me when I sat with them.

"Why not use the big cages outside?" I asked Rex one day. "We could squirt them out easier."

"We used to. You can't keep neighborhood kids from sneaking around, sticking their arms inside."

"The monkeys seem so tame, even Big Man."

He shook his head. "One time Mack grabbed a handful of a girl's hair. He just wanted to smell her shampoo—he does that—but he's so strong. She told her parents he tried to scalp her. The father came back with a gun. Lucky I was home."

"That's crazy."

"Yeah, but when they get that look, like a war going on inside, watch out. One second everything is nice, nice, love, love—and the next, 'Must bite! Must bite!' flashes in their eyes."

"They're always so sweet to me."

"So far. You can't predict when somebody will get jealous or want one of us for himself. Especially Big Man."

Within a couple months, I was doing more than my share of the work, but hey, it was appreciated. By the third month, things started to get a little tedious. Rex had been unemployed for a couple of years, living on the investments. Now with me around, or so he said, we were running short. I wondered why he hadn't figured that out earlier. He didn't ask me to go back to work, but the Mercedes was on lease, and it had to be turned in. We were stuck with the old pickup that was used for carting the monkeys in cages to the vet and bringing home bags of feed.

Rex started giving sailing lessons at the Yacht Club. Now he was gone most of the day, and every morning during prime feeding time. "Not working" was far more labor than I had imagined. I didn't know his finances were so tight or I might have had second thoughts about the deal. Still, I got to drink piña coladas and sunbathe all afternoon on my own private beach.

Sometimes my best girlfriend from the club would come by to keep up her all-over tan. Danielle was luscious with her tiny shaved mound and vanilla double-Ds. We'd loll naked on a quilt on the little beach, sucking face and pressing our tits together until somebody's fingers, usually mine, would rove over tender skin. I'd open her like an envelope, with one finger, and let the breeze dry her pink edges, so I could tongue them wet again. We ordered in, pizza or sushi, and by sundown we'd have rubbed ourselves raw. Rex had met her, and must've figured we fooled around, being dancer types, but he never said anything. I gave him whatever he wanted.

At first, we went out to dinner most nights. There was so much food prep for the monkeys that the whole day would be taken up by food if we cooked dinner. There were lots of nice seafood places, and we had our favorites. At night, we'd sit at the huge window overlooking our bay and listen to music, gazing out at the stars and the water. He had a spotlight behind the house so we could see the palms blowing and the sparkle of waves. On the first night of a full moon, he turned the light off and we sat there in the dark and waited for the moon to come up. It cast its glittery trail across the water, and I thought it was a magic road leading right to me, where I had found my jackpot.

Sometimes we'd put on Mack's leash and take him out with us behind the house, where he could be fastened to a rail left from the tourist attraction days. He really enjoyed the fresh air, and he would sit in a palm that slanted near the edge of the water. He'd flirt, throwing me kisses, and I'd unhook him and let him cuddle next to me and pick through my hair.

Our eating at nice places and star-gazing got less and less over the weeks and months. Rex started to watch TV sports in the den a few nights a week. Sometimes he went out with his buddies, leaving me there to sip my drink and count the stars alone.

One night I thought one of the spiders was using another as a punching bag. When I checked, Itsy and Bitsy were grooming each other, Mack and Sweetums were swinging, and Big Man was racked out in the other room playing with his toe. The door between the rooms was closed as we generally left it. They all looked up at me, like, "What's your problem?" I think they could hear my footsteps, or see me in their mirrors. It was all a trick to get my attention.

These ruckuses began to break out more in both rooms. I'd go in to check on them and scratch backs, bring treats. Mack or Big Man would often sit there and masturbate, looking me straight in the eye. Sometimes the females would finger themselves.

I could sign a few phrases I'd learned to Big Man, but he just stared at me. He was stubborn. They were bored,

poor things, him especially, because he was smarter and
more isolated. I wanted to swing with them and get some
exercise, but when I mentioned it to Rex he said that was
too dangerous if he wasn't home. I knew he was right. I saw
them when the softness in their eyes turned flat and hard,
like there was something wild ready to break out. That's
when I'd race for the door.

Rex went out two nights in a row one week and I was
really pissed. He had an old friend down from Miami, but
I was almost mad enough to head over to Reefers and see
some of the regulars. I started to get dressed and then I
thought about them—the regulars—and remembered
the smell of that place. I wasn't that angry. Big Man was
making a racket as usual, so I pulled a chair into the hall
where he could see me to quiet him down. I knew the
best way to stop boredom, so I slipped off my shorts and
panties and put my favorite finger on my button and gave
myself a nice twinge. Big Man seemed to know what I was
doing. His eyebrows went up and he whimpered. When I
started to breathe hard, he began to huff. He was jacking
off, standing on the other side of the door. I wondered if
this was a bad idea, but I didn't stop. I was almost there.
I came and moaned out loud, and Big Man wasn't far
behind. I was glad I hadn't left him alone. He was my
friend.

I put on my shorts and got another drink. Big Man
was whining, so I took a look and decided to let him out.
He was calm, and he knew what the leash meant, so it
was no problem to hook him up and lead him to the back
patio. After he sat for a while in his palm, he came down
to sit on the bottom of the lounge chair and I gave him
pieces of ice from my drink. He stood behind my back and

groomed me. I don't know what he found there, but his
cool fingers picking through my hair was like a massage.
We both enjoyed it. I wasn't sure if Rex would like the idea,
so I didn't tell him. It wasn't like Big Man would try to
escape. He'd been born in captivity and he knew where his
meals came from. He was more civilized than most of the
regulars at Reefers. It became our little secret. Every time
Rex left, Big Man got out.

As the nights turned cooler toward Christmas, Big
Man would sit next to me and doze off with his head on
my chest. He'd wake up drowsy and look at my face. Nice,
nice! glowed in his round eyes. But the animal was always
close. Sometimes he'd jump, as if I'd hit him, and his lips
would curl back. Must bite! Must bite! was fighting to take
over his brain. I'd get out of his way until he settled down.
He wasn't so different from the guys at the bar. You never
knew with men.

I started to get suspicious of Rex. He didn't have much
time for sex or monkey tricks, started spending every
day at the Yacht Club. Since the snowbirds were down, it
made sense that he had more work, but I thought he might
be seeing another woman. If you think it, it's true, they
always say. Maybe she was a snowbird, and this was their
yearly rendezvous. I had my own girlfriend, but I didn't
like that Rex was sneaking around and leaving me home
peeling bananas. I wondered if that was his plan all along,
find some sucker for the monkeys so he could be with his
girlfriend. Maybe she didn't like monkeys and I was his
chance to make a break. Maybe that was what his wife did
to him.

The difference was that Julia had money. She left him
with investments and the house, and still had enough

dough to take off. He was pretty much stuck with me, unless he wanted to leave with nothing. I started to think I could do without him fine, but even if he left me with the place, finances would be lousy. I'd have to take care of the monkeys and go back to spreading my ass.

Finally, one night Rex stayed home with me, and we had a drink on the patio like the old days. I had several drinks. Big Man was making a ruckus inside, and I knew why, but Rex ignored it.

I was unhappy to see Rex finish eating, make himself another scotch and get comfortable back out on the lounge chair without a word of thanks for the dinner I'd made. I sat down on his lap anyway, giving it one more cheerleader try. I massaged the back of his neck, licked at his lips, and ground my ass a little into his groin. But he kissed back without pressure, his eyes glazed. I sucked on his neck and he pushed my face away, going back to shallow kisses, his arms straight at his sides, hands flat on the couch. Things had changed, but it wasn't my fault. I gave up.

I didn't make an issue of it because I didn't want to hear any lies. I tried to act normal and talk about all the cute things the monkeys did that day. Then I asked an important question. "What will the monkeys do if something happens to us?"

"I guess you'll be here when I'm gone," he said.

"Great. I can't handle them."

He took a drink of his scotch. "Don't worry. I have a big life insurance policy. You can get any help you need. These guys could live to be forty."

"Forty! How much money?"

"A million. My wife set that up too, so the monkeys would be taken care of, no matter what."

"That was pretty generous, but if they live till forty—"

"She has plenty of money. She felt responsible for these guys, even though she hated them."

"Hated them?"

"Yeah, I don't know why. Big Man scared her one time, and she never forgave him."

"What did he do?"

"Nothing. She said he was *going* to do something."

I figured Julie just wanted out. If you had money everything was easy.

We both kept drinking. It was the only thing we enjoyed together anymore, but it made me hostile.

"So what are the monkeys and me supposed to do all the time when you're gone?"

"Shh. You're too loud."

"So what? Nobody around here."

"You'll wake them."

I got louder on purpose. "Well, they're in this too."

He whispered. "I have to work. Somebody has to."

"You don't make much."

"I don't wave my naked ass in anybody's face."

"You sure?"

He gave me a disgusted look. I didn't ask again. It didn't matter what he was doing. It was how he tricked me, setting me up to think he had money, forcing me into the boring shit job he was sick of.

After that night, the million bucks wouldn't leave me alone. It taunted me every morning when I cut vegetables, and all afternoon when I scrubbed shit off the walls and windows, slimy lettuce from the floor, washed sour soggy monkey biscuit out of all the water bowls, and scraped yogurt and oatmeal from the windowsill. After about a week I realized that, although Rex was a lot older, I couldn't hold out till he died. Nothing was the way it was supposed to be. I was cheap help for a man trapped with wild children who would never grow up.

I started my training plan, concentrating on Big Man because he could do the job alone, and the others would follow his lead. I had our wedding picture blown up huge, and cut Rex's face out of it to mount it with a stick inside a shirt and jeans that I got out of the dirty laundry. I stuffed the clothes with Rex's underwear. I padded the stick with foam rubber so it looked like a neck, and put an "X" on the left side where the jugular would be. I sewed a set of cock and balls to attach inside the pants.

I fried up a pound of bacon, and put it into the refrigerator, knowing the shit was going to fly when I started doing the rewarding. I coaxed Big Man into the kitchen on his leash, signing, "Bacon, bacon, Big Man." I had a strip inside the oven, and I stood in front of it with the dummy. "Big Man, bite," I said and signed it to him. I pointed to the X and signed it again and again. "Big Man, bite."

His head moved high and low from side to side. He sniffed to find the bacon, but the whole room was filled with the smell. I held the dummy near his face and signed "Bite," pointing to the X. "Bite," I signed, "I give bacon."

I signed "bite and bacon," "bite and bacon," but he didn't get it, or pretended not to. I was aggravated. I took the dummy and bit it on the X, shaking my head like a shark in a frenzy. I opened the oven and grabbed the bacon to flop it on the dummy's neck. I shoved it at Big Man and he bit lightly—all he wanted was the bacon—but it was a start.

I opened the refrigerator to get another piece. Big mistake. Big Man grabbed the platter and pushed me down. The leash came right out of my hand. He sat on the floor and ate the whole pound in thirty seconds. I realized I had little control.

The next day I hooked Big Man outside. I wanted him to know that the bacon was all mine and he would only get it if he did what I said.

I brought out the bacon and set it on a table beyond his reach. He went wild. He jerked at the chain and his eyes bounced from me to the bacon and back. I dug into the back of the broom closet and got the dummy and stood there signing and saying, "Big Man, bite. I give bacon."

He started making his hooting chimp noises, trying to coax me, full of glee.

"What does Big Man want?" I said. "Tell Darlene," I signed.

He continued to hoot and I held the dummy near him. "Kill Rex, get bacon," I said. "Kill Rex!" I handed him the dummy but not the bacon. "Bite Rex!" I held out a strip. "Kill Rex!"

Finally, he curled back his lips and ripped a chunk out of the rubber. I grabbed two strips of bacon and stuck them at him. He shoved them into his mouth. Then he dug in and ripped every shred of rubber off the dummy's neck.

We went on half the day that way, with several repaired necks, moving down to the genitals, until I could barely say the word *bite* and he'd have his teeth on the dummy tearing the rubber away. After he'd shredded all the parts, I let him rip out the stuffing and toss it around.

His animal nature was taking control. I played up my role as his pal, chaining him in the kitchen one day, giving him all my attention. He sat on a chair and watched me wash and cut fruit and vegetables all morning. After a while, I heard him make a familiar grunt, and when I turned, he was pumping his cock. His eyes were soft and his lips were curled in a smile as he came on the seat of the kitchen chair. He was with me all the way.

I decided the best way to do it was in one big rush. I'd unlock the doors while Rex was having his coffee and wait for Big Man to find his way into the kitchen when I started frying the bacon. I'd sign "Kill Rex," behind his back, and in the few seconds that Rex had to live, he'd think he was meeting his natural fate, the fate he deserved for betraying his children. The county would take all the monkeys away, most likely destroy them, but I tried not to think of that. I'd be free with the million. Nobody would suspect me. The crazy guy with the monkeys had been asking for it for years.

I didn't waste any time. That afternoon I put the dummy clothes in the wash and threw the foam rubber in the trash, burned the photo face. Nobody would be able put all that together.

The next morning Rex was sitting at the kitchen table, reading the paper. I'd unlocked the cage doors while the monkeys were still asleep. I told Rex I felt like making some bacon and eggs. As soon as I said the word, the hooting started. Big Man went wild and the others followed. Rex shook his head and kept reading.

The bacon barely started to crackle when Big Man came leaping through the door. I don't think he even saw me sign. He knocked Rex to the floor and bit into his throat, tearing away flesh easier than he had the rubber. Blood shot out and he kept on biting. Rex dropped,

unconscious in seconds. It was more horrible than I'd
imagined. Big Man moved down and tore up his cock and
balls, yanking them off with his hand, ripping the sack with
his teeth. I was frozen.

Big Man didn't forget the bacon. He looked at me and
I jumped aside, and he picked up the half-cooked pieces
three at a time and stuffed them into his bloody mouth.
Mack, Sweetums, Itsy, and Bitsy were in the doorway
watching, excited. I started toward the door to make my
break down the stairs. Big Man finished with the bacon,
and he leaped to block the way, with Must bite! in his eyes.
I grabbed a sharp knife off the sink, but he reached for
my wrist and twisted. The knife fell to the floor. "Bacon!"
I yelled and pointed toward the stove. He turned and let
loose, and I ran the opposite direction into the monkey
rooms and slammed the door, to wait until they'd all
settled down.

I didn't count on Big Man locking me in.

Caged for hours, I was at their mercy. I had to pee in
the corner. I wasn't anywhere near as strong as they were,
and obviously no smarter, because there was no hope
unless somebody came to the house. I thought they might
get bored eventually and let me out, take care of me, as
I had taken care of them, but they seemed to have no
interest.

They were all banging around in the kitchen—no
doubt, eating all the food, tossing pans, breaking dishes,
and yanking out drawers. After a long time, things got
quiet. I woke up at dusk. Big Man's face was at the window.
Maybe he wanted me to fix the yogurt and oatmeal. I went
to the door. "Big Man, let Darlene out," I said and signed.
"Big Man, unlock door."

He looked at me and got a big grin, pulling his lips out, snorting and mocking me. His hands came close to the window and he moved his fingers. I couldn't believe it. The chimp was signing. "Darlene kill Rex."

"No!" I signed, "Big Man kill Rex!"

He started with that chimp laugh that made my skin crawl, a piercing mocking hoot. "Darlene kill Rex," he signed and laughed. He bent down then, and I thought he was unlocking the door. I wasn't sure I wanted out. But that wasn't it. His face came back up and he was holding the sharp knife in his teeth by the blade. It was covered in Rex's blood. "Darlene kill Rex."

My guts froze. The handle of the knife had my prints on it. But it was impossible that he could know that, a coincidence how he was holding it. I had to get that knife. I kicked the door and banged with my fists, and he ran off. I sat down on the floor, drained and horrified. But then the door opened slightly. Big Man had unlocked it. I looked out. Nobody there. No knife. I didn't think the police knew sign language or would even listen to a chimp, but they would take the knife for evidence. As the beneficiary of a million bucks, I was in trouble.

The spiders were lounging all over the couch. Groggy, greedy monkeys, limbs dangling. Liquor fumes were thick, and bottles broken, so they might've been drinking. There were gummy bears and peanut shells ground into piles of crap on the carpet, a banana peel hanging on a lamp shade. I walked past it all into the kitchen. Garbage, blood, and shit were everywhere. The refrigerator was open and empty, milk and orange juice cartons smashed, pickles and ketchup and lettuce trampled on the tile floor. They'd eaten at least two days worth of carrots, celery, bananas,

oranges. A fifty pound bag of monkey biscuit was dumped
in the corner and somebody had peed on it.

A river of blood showed Rex's body had been dragged
under the table. I looked and held my breath. Besides the
torn and bitten flesh of his neck there were clearly knife
wounds, the throat slit from the right ear to the mangled,
stringy part on the left, the head nearly severed. I gagged
up the bile in my stomach. Everything was wrong. I wanted
Rex back. He hadn't been so bad. I heard something
behind me and stood up. Big Man walked in and signed,
"Darlene kill Rex."

"Where's the knife, Big Man?"

He started to hoot. He'd been waiting for his chance.
He was playing me, just like I'd thought I was playing
him, and Rex had played me. I bent over and gagged some
more. Big Man stared. He kept laughing until the animal
look came into his eyes. He pulled his cock and it grew
out long and hard. I jerked with the impulse to run, but I
had to find that knife. He sat on the chair and worked his
pud. All I needed to do was wipe off my prints. Without
evidence, nobody would believe a freaking ape.

I got down on my hands and knees and raked through
the slimy trash with my fingers. The knife could be
anywhere. I tried to think like an ape, but my brain was
dead. I would never find it like that. Big Man was too
smart. The only way was to convince him to show me,
himself. I didn't have much time.

Big Man was rocking and grunting; his come squirted
out onto the chair. He nodded off and I let him doze for a
few minutes while I took a last useless look around. Then I
stood across the room and called his name.

"Darlene wants knife," I signed and shouted. "Darlene

wants knife." I turned my back to him, slipped my shorts and panties down, and bent over. It always worked with men—or so I'd thought. "Darlene loves Big Man," I said. I bent farther and signed between my legs. He grinned and hooted, showing his mouthful of long yellow teeth and dark gums. I had his attention.

I bit my lip and sucked up what I had left of pride. If Big Man was smart enough to hide the knife, we could make a deal. "Get knife," I signed. I pushed my finger inside myself to be sure he got the message. He bounded on top of me in a second and I clenched my cheeks, prepared to be nailed from behind, like I'd seen the monkeys doing it, but he spun me around and opened his gap of a rotten mouth and plastered it over my face. He'd been watching me and Rex. His teeth cut into my nose and chin, and the hot stench of broccoli breath poured over me. I convulsed hard and broke loose, jerking my head back and ejecting a slug of phlegmy bile that landed on his furred thigh. He snatched it up quick, cupped it into his mouth, and swallowed it down like an oyster appetizer, then pulled my small frame forward onto his penis. It tore in, pointy and hard, like a knife. Knife. I wished it was the fucking knife. He huffed and drooled onto my face. How many times would I have to fuck him to get the murder weapon?

Big Man finished with a long grunt, knocked me sideways to the floor, stepped on my throat, and dashed out of the room. I choked and gasped. Any more weight on that foot and he'd have broken my windpipe. I must have blacked out because it was dark when I opened my eyes.

No Big Man. No knife. I dragged myself up and walked through the hall to the living room. I could hear him in there messing around. Moonlight from the window

showed him cross-legged in the corner. I snapped on
the light. He was finger-painting with crap on the wall.
No knife. He turned and looked at me. His shitty hand
dropped to his lap. His prick was hard. It dawned on me
then, that I had no elongated vagina. Big Man would rape
me whenever he pleased. I turned and ran for the door, but
he leaped onto my back and pinned me to the floor. My
face hit the hard tile and my teeth cut through my lip. His
pointy knife ripped into my ass. It wasn't worth a million.

Cold-Blooded Lovers

The day he flushed his meds and purchased a dress for his iguana, Gregory Waxman's real problems were over. He had stopped taking the drugs a week or more prior— time becoming somewhat fluid. He bid the pills final *bon voyage* after his wife admitted, without apology, that she had started having an affair and planned to continue it: "Waxman, (she never called him Greg anymore) I have needs." He was without reply because he had no feelings about it, no hot blood running through his veins. Since he had reached his mid-fifties, he often felt just a model of his former self —perhaps a natural state of aging, or else ten years of marriage had taken a toll.

Greta's affair was an unexpected development because he had never heard about these "needs," as opposed to the common harangues on his poor housekeeping skills and low-paying adjunct College English job, despite the fact that his family's investments had paid for the professionally landscaped four-bedroom home with heated pool and Jacuzzi. Greta worked as an administrative assistant at Ft. Lauderdale City Hall and put in a half share on the bills, so she had developed a sense of entitlement.

In practical terms, nothing would change, since she wasn't making any plans to leave. At least, now he knew what she'd been doing when she stayed out half the night. Accepting the new twist in their relationship was relatively easy since Greta's "needs" did not involve him, and he was free to utilize his summer break however he so desired in satisfying neglected desires of his own.

His pleasure that day was to finish writing a short story, fix a grilled cheese, and drive to the high-class pet boutique in the Galleria Mall that stocked iguana attire, Linguina in tow.

On a lark, he had investigated stylish day and evening wear in sizes to fit iguanas and ferrets, but until recently hadn't known that Linguina desired apparel. Since iguanas have no external sex organs, to Waxman, clothing seemed a needless restriction. In fact, until she started commenting on Greta's sleek business suits, he wasn't entirely sure of Linguina's gender, although she had always seemed feminine. However, having matured from the skinny electric-green infant that curled around his hand and wrist, as flexible as a noodle, to a slender four-foot "dinosaur" with shapely hips, she had begun to request pretty things, and there was no doubt from her slim build as she approached maturity that she was a young lady.

He saw no reason to refuse her, an only-child. Since his plans didn't include introducing her to those wild iguanas in the neighborhood, there was no worry of future costs for a lavish wedding. He would, however, consider a bat mitzvah or a quinceañera when she reached fifteen, which, as he determined in iguana years, would be soon. He and Greta had attended several of those occasions, and it seemed only right to garner some gifts for Linguina.

He lifted Linguina from the dashboard where she loved to bask, and draped her across the tops of his shoulders.

He knew they made quite the picture with Linguina's shiny green form curled around his neck, enhancing a sallow Mr. Clean look with his smooth-shaved bald head. She settled with her chin on his clavicle. He had handled her daily since childhood, and she often rode around the house on him and down the street when he went for a newspaper. The neighbors referred to Waxman as Iguana Man, and truth be told, he enjoyed his reputation.

The clerk looked up from her novel and waved as he walked past her to the aisle with iguana clothes.

"So," he said to Linguina, "You'll need some cool and casual outfits for everyday and one or two fancy party dresses." He lifted her onto the counter next to the selection of soft cotton tees in pink, lavender, and aqua. There were also animal print shirts in tiger, leopard, and giraffe, some with rhinestones around the necks or fur collars. He picked up a silky pink dress sewn with sparkling crystals down the torso.

"Those are Swarovski." The clerk was at the end of the aisle watching.

He didn't know what she meant and didn't care. Too expensive. He stuffed the dress under the stack, hoping to avoid Linguina's gaze, and turned to the casual selections.

Black leather vests bore Harley Davidson insignias. Apparently, the style was bottomless. He gave Linguina a little push so that she could select her favorites, but the cold air-conditioning had already made her sluggish. He empathized, feeling chilled and stiff himself, and made a quick pick of a lavender sundress and a sailor-girl outfit with pleated skirt. "No Harley crap for my girl," he told her. She didn't object, but he could see tears in her eyes. "Oh, all right." He noted the $115 price tag, but Linguina was

already giggling. Hell, Greta wouldn't balk at charging a
pair of earrings for that amount, and he never splurged on
his own clothing.

"Do you want nighties and lounge wear?"

Linguina said she did, and he chose a flowered cotton
gown for everyday use and a gold satin backless with
a matching robe for moonlit nights on the patio. The
gold would shine beautifully with her coloring. He was
beginning to worry about her temperature, so he quickly
selected evening wear: a slinky silver v-necked shift and
a tiger print halter top with a sleek matching skirt. There
were boots, running shoes, and evening slippers farther
down the aisle, but he would save those for another time
and take her home to try on all her new clothes.

Waxman couldn't wait to show off his lovely daughter.
That night she selected the tiger print evening outfit, and
he drove down to Lincoln Road in Miami, famous for its
outdoor mall with cafes, where dogs nearly equaled the
number of people, and he had seen shoulders decorated
with parrots and anacondas. He chose the Universe Café,
since they served much vegetarian fare. Linguina had
eaten her day's portion of grated yellow squash mixed with
soaked monkey biscuit that morning, but perhaps she
might pick around on some hummus.

As he strolled, Waxman noted the South Beach crowd.
There was a guy with a ring through his nose like a bull.
Who could guess what other rings he had under his
clothing? Tattoos and piercings were everywhere, blue hair,
pants hanging off butts revealing undershorts, women's
cracks exposed by tight low-cut spandex, enormous
breasts bursting over lacey negligee tops. Who knew what
acts they performed in the privacy of their homes, if this

was their public appearance? He and Linguina were the most conservative pair in sight. Linguina's evening wear could even be called traditional.

They took a table under a tall potted palm. The first people to pass by were lavish with compliments. The halter top came across under Linguina's armpits, tying in back to expose her lovely lower torso, and the skirt fit her waist perfectly, tapering to her slim, muscular thighs. She straightened her front legs and raised her head tall, taking it all in and enjoying the petting of her frill and stroking of her beaded skin. Running fingers along Linguina's ribs was like feeling coins through a fine mesh change purse, and everyone wanted to do it.

When they were alone he lowered her to the table and asked if she was having a good time. She said she couldn't think of anything she'd rather do than dress up and go out on the town with him. It was exactly what he wanted to hear. He kissed her head, then picked up the drink menu, thinking about a martini for himself and maybe a virgin piña colada for Linguina. She had never tasted pineapple and coconut.

"I'm sorry, sir, but iguanas aren't permitted on the tables—even a fashion model like yours."

His nasal intonation had a sarcastic twang, and Waxman had to control his anger. He motioned the waiter to the side away from Linguina. "Please, you'll insult my daughter," he whispered. He pointed to three dogs leashed nearby. "Look at them, noisy, shedding animals that take up half the sidewalk, as opposed to my lovely little girl who adds elegance and chic to any table. This is some kind of discrimination."

"Salmonella discrimination, sir. State law. If you set

your lizard in the planter, I can serve you."

Waxman jumped out of his chair. "I won't put my
daughter in the dirt in her new dress!" Staring back at
the waiter, he picked up Linguina and placed her on his
shoulders. "You can bet we won't be eating here again."
He held onto her fore and hind legs and performed a little
twirl, ending in a pirouette before he stalked off. South
Beach was not as open-minded as one would guess.

They spent a while strolling and retrieved their good
mood with the many appreciative glances and amazed
oohs and ahhs. Waxman bought a mango gelato in a sugar
cone, since she loved mango, but Linguina wouldn't touch
it. Probably too cold. He sat down on a bench near a
fountain. Linguina slung her tail across his chest, put her
mouth close to his right ear, and whispered that she didn't
think of him as her father.

His head jerked toward her and her tongue whipped
out and slid along his temple. He knew what she meant,
without question, and it was everything he could have
hoped for. The notion of being her father had been
mistakenly formed on the basis of size and dependency.
He pulled a napkin from his pocket and dabbed gelato
from the tip of his nose. Linguina's eyes were shining. She
was his true love and loved him in return. All this time he
had been too straight-laced to admit it to himself.

He grasped at a way to describe his feelings to her. This
was nothing like the love he felt for Greta, far superior,
more elegant, eternal. "*Agave*" he told Linguina, "—no,
that's the tequila plant." She never corrected him, but he
wanted to get it right. "*Agape*," he finally came up with. "It's
a Greek word meaning selfless, spiritual love, based on
wonder and amazement." He pressed her face against his

ear as a tender embrace. No matter that their bodies were so different as to prohibit a sexual relationship, he didn't need that. *Agape* was more powerful than any physical love he had ever experienced.

His realization opened the floodgates, and over the next few weeks Waxman devoted all his time to Linguina, getting up early to search the neighborhood bushes for the yellow hibiscus that she craved, taking her to the boutique many afternoons so that she had a different shirt and evening gown for every day of the week and several bikinis, purchasing exotic fruits and music that soothed her. She stopped trying to conceal her feelings and it became clear that her amazement and wonder for the world increased with the attention he paid her.

When Greta informed him that she was taking a two-week cruise, Waxman lost all inhibitions. He invested in a larger cage, the most luxurious he could find, an eight-foot high hexagonal with a diameter of five feet, in black wrought iron with various levels of artificial branches for perching and a waterfall in the bottom with its own filtering system. He knew Greta would scream when she saw it and again when the $4,000 charge came in, but the "habitat" was actually on sale for thirty percent off, and she would get over it. What choice did she have anyway? He bought extra sun lamps and heat rocks so that Linguina had various comfortable and healthy places to lounge. Letting her have the run of the porch would have been preferable, but her nails would rip through the thin screening, so she could only stay loose with supervision.

Instead of sleeping in the guest room, where he had taken up residence, Waxman began spending his nights in the hammock on the screened porch, so he could be near

Linguina's cage, and she could wake him if she wanted
out. The heat and humidity took getting used to, but when
he felt gluey, he just cooled off in the pool. High wooden
privacy fences had been built by both neighbors, and
Waxman had connected a short piece on each side and
a gate to create his own private paradise. He had left the
back end open to a field and small woods to allow visits
from raccoons, opossums, and foxes. Beyond the woods
was a park, so the yard felt rural and isolated, even though
downtown and the beach were only a few miles away. He
had the Jacuzzi installed when he and Greta got married, in
hopes that she would enjoy spending time with him there,
but it hadn't worked out.

Linguina, however, found the yard fascinating with the
squabbling monk parakeets in the palms and darting anole
lizards, as well as occasional furry visitors that came in
from the back. He brought his desk and laptop outside and
positioned them near her cage, so he would be close to her
and enjoy the occasional glance at her beauty as he read,
wrote stories, and went online.

One morning he spotted a wild iguana in back. He had
seen several in the neighborhood and previously noted
this fellow's calling card, a wet cigar-like turd left on the
same stepping stone each day for over a week. It was a
mud-colored beast with a splash of orange, built sturdy,
no doubt a male, with puffed jowls, prizefighter shoulders
and thick limbs and tail covered in hide like an elephant's.
Linguina was already changed from her jammies into the
black leather Harley vest, and the male was giving her the
eye. She seemed unimpressed, perhaps not even aware,
but Waxman wondered if a flirtation might develop. For a
moment he pondered whether he was depriving her of the

natural experience of mating and motherhood, but she had
been born in captivity and raised without reptilian contact.
It would be dangerous for her to mix with the riffraff where
she might contract diseases. Besides, it would destroy
him to see her writhing with a neighborhood ruffian. He
dashed outside and ran the intruder out of the yard all the
way back into the field.

They spent most afternoons lounging and taking
dips in the pool. Waxman often dozed naked in a floating
chair with a guava juice and rum, a drink Linguina would
tongue on occasion while she stretched full length on his
stomach bestowing kisses and light nudges of her snout to
his chin. It was a shame for her not to wear her bikinis, but
swimming with fabric hindered the graceful serpentine
movements of her body, and she preferred the warmth of
his skin against hers while sunbathing.

Waxman guessed that Greta would find his activities
unwholesome, but who was she to throw stones? Anyway,
she paid little attention to household matters and less
to him. Waxman figured that her lover must be married.
Otherwise, he couldn't see a reason for her to stay on at the
house.

Of course, the guy might be playing her for the short
term. Waxman knew intellectually, or remembered, that
Greta, barely over forty, was quite the blonde bombshell.
However, with his new sense of beauty, he perceived
the softness of her breasts and rounded buttocks to be
less sensuous than slabs of suet, whereas he remained in
rapture for hours gazing at Linguina's crisp leathery armor,
tight over her ribs, tapered hips, and slender tail. She was
his inspiration to live that Greta had never been.

Their affection continued to grow and they invented

new ways to express it. When Linguina was settled on a convenient perch, Waxman would run his palm down her frill, his finger and thumb caressing her delicate hide from head to tail until she had completely relaxed. Then he would kiss the folded skin of her armpits and legpits and rub his nose against her ribs. When she felt frisky, Linguina would nip him on his chest or arms and neck, love bites that he had learned to enjoy despite the small chinks she took out with her bony mouth. He scolded her playfully about being wild, but didn't want to hurt her feelings. His torso and arms were taking on a mottled look from lasting discoloration, but he didn't care. Lately, he sometimes felt that his life was only fiction being held together by his point of view, but the story was idyllic, so why question it?

About a week after the first iguana's visit, three more appeared. Two were degenerate creatures close in size to the mud-colored one, only less orange and a greenish-brown, the third a slender gray-blue female companion. Mr. Mud sat the closest to the screen. A bright orange flap of skin the shape of a Chinese fan opened and closed below his jaw, a mating display. The set-up hit Waxman instantly; the thin pretty one was their moll and Mud, the dominant male, getting tired of sharing, was on the prowl for Linguina. She saw them too and craned her neck to get a good look at all four. He wondered if she thought of herself as competition. Of course, Linguina put the other female to shame. Her interest upset him. The males looked tough and frightening, but as soon as he opened the screen door, they took off, scrambling through the grass into the weeds and out of sight in the woods. He knew that escaped iguanas had bred to the point of being called a menace, so there were probably many in the vicinity.

He began to worry. He had seen Linguina scratching in the corner of her cage, repeating the same movement of her arms over and over, even though she wasn't accomplishing anything on the metal bars and floor. Was it some kind of frustrated mating behavior, an attempt to dig a nest? Her appetite had fallen off also. Something was wrong, but she insisted she was fine. Didn't want to hurt his feelings. He had read that if there is a habitat problem, animals develop stereotypies, compulsive repetitious behaviors, so that might be the case. He resolved to spend less time reading and writing in order to provide more freedom and amusement for her.

Linguina enjoyed music, especially The Doors, so he bought new speakers that looked like rocks and placed them on all four sides of the patio to get a concert-hall effect combined with a natural setting. He also purchased a karaoke machine since she had expressed pleasure in hearing him sing, and they enjoyed crooning together. The neighbors on both sides were snowbirds, never around during summer, so he played the music as loud as she wanted.

One afternoon, nude following a swim, Linguina on Waxman's shoulders, they were practicing a dance to "People Are Strange." Waxman had installed the mirror from the dresser on the outside wall so he could watch Linguina keeping time with her head bobs and tail whips. He planned to make a video for YouTube and blow that silly Snowball the Cockatoo out of the water.

Greta stuck her head out the sliding door and hollered. "Waxman! Waxman, have you lost your—" She covered her mouth as she saw them dancing before the mirror.

He thought she might have gagged. He sang softly to

Linguina: "Greta is strange . . . cause she's a stranger . . . her face looks ugly, when she's at home." He thought, hell, why can't we all get along? He did a twirl ending in a pirouette. "Lost my pants?" he yelled back. "No." He pointed toward the house. "Saving on laundry!"

Greta tried to deflate his mood, her eyes searing from under hooded brows. "Is this your plan to get me back?" she hollered. Her voice sounded hopeful. He wondered if the boyfriend was no more.

He blasted the volume for the chorus. . . . *"CAUSE SHE'S STRANGE."* Linguina dug her claws into his neck. "Sorry!" He turned down the volume. "Get you back? Linguina is my true love!"

He danced to the end of the pool, and around the far side still singing to show Linguina that the spat was all in jest and anything Greta had to say was meaningless. "No worries," he whispered into the general area where her ears would be, but Linguina was still tense, her claws sunk in deep. He knew some of her nails would break off and remain lodged. He hoped she could grow them back.

Greta was staring, shaking her head.

He sang and danced his way down the steps into the shallow end and started detaching claws one by one from his throat. Two nails remained stuck near his clavicle. He crouched down to put Linguina on the edge of the pool so she could scamper to her cage, safe from Greta, then he got out and walked over to the small chest of drawers where he stored her outfits.

Greta's eyes darted one way and another, taking in the cage, the hammock and Waxman sorting through the little clothes, her face convulsing slightly, as if she were confused.

He selected a light peach sundress, slipped it under Linguina's arms, and zipped it up the back. He still felt affection for Greta, but he understood the problem now. Their "love" had been based on needs instead of wonder, so when their needs evolved separately the love disintegrated. The bond between Waxman and Linguina was pure and everlasting *agape*. Before her, he never understood the difference. Now he was at peace. There were a few loose caps on Linguina's frill and he picked them off. "My sweetie is starting to molt," he told her. He sang a few more lines, bellowing out the word *strange*. It was all in fun.

Greta turned off the music and stood with her arms crossed. "I'm calling the lawyer."

Waxman had found more caps to groom from Linguina's frill and didn't look up.

"Did you hear me?"

An idle threat. He'd heard them before. He wished she would just go live with the guy and enjoy herself. He could manage to pay the bills. Turning off the air-conditioning alone would save a bundle. Then he could open up the whole house to Linguina. "Take any furniture you want," he said. "I'll probably redecorate."

Something pottery hit the tile. "Get real! Do you think I'm going to let you have the house?"

He didn't give her the satisfaction of looking to see what she had broken. "I guess not, but it's my house, so if anybody is leaving, it's you."

"Don't be so damned sure, Mr. Iguana Man. Ever heard of the Baker Act?"

Of course he had, but he didn't flinch.

When the sliding door slammed shut, he kissed

Linguina on top of her head. He had promised a visit to
the shops on the beach, but now he was worried. Greta
might be able to convince his psychiatrist, or even a cop,
to recommend involuntary inpatient placement. He would
be halfway to the Florida State Hospital if she subpoenaed
documentation of his paranoid schizophrenia, no matter
that he had completely recovered. She would also have
to show that he was likely to harm himself or others, but
harm was such a subjective word. He looked at his bruised
and damaged forearms, felt the fresh scab on his chin.
Love bites. It would seem obvious that Greta was trying
to put him away in order to keep the house for her and her
boyfriend, but you could never be sure about experts and
judges. Greta was cunning. She might even call in PETA
with some kind of ridiculous sexual abuse charge involving
Linguina.

It couldn't hurt to be safe, even if these thoughts were
only paranoia trying to resurface. He decided not to alarm
Linguina by mentioning his fears, but apologized, saying
he felt too ill to go out, and changed her into her flowered
nighty. She looked sad, but he picked a half dozen yellow
hibiscus and left her calmly eating as he went to the garage
to find a deadbolt for the front door and a padlock for
inside the back gate.

As he screwed the bolt from the old rabbit hutch
into the woodwork, he realized it was flimsy, but at least,
Greta couldn't sneak up on him anymore. She wouldn't
choose to trudge through the woods and scrub, picking up
sandspurs and poison ivy. Greta didn't like to sweat off her
mascara.

He was napping in his hammock with Linguina, in the
heat of late afternoon, when they were awakened by noisy

battering. "Waxman? Let me in!" Greta on a rampage at the side gate. "I know you're back there. Open up!"

"Sir, open up, please." So, she had brought the cops. "Sir? We just want to talk."

He set Linguina on her perch and pulled on a pair of shorts. She was wearing her Harley vest, her favorite attire, as requested, and he wondered if the biker style would make a bad impression, but he didn't want to upset her.

"For god's sake, Waxman, open the gate! We're here to help you!" Greta making good on her threat.

A megaphone boomed out from the front. "COME OUT, MR. WAXMAN. WE DON'T WANT TO BREAK DOWN YOUR DOOR."

His door—those were the operative words as far as he was concerned.

"Gregory, we're not going to hurt you. Just come out." It was his last psychiatrist. Greta had brought her minions. The boyfriend was probably there too, saying "Nice house, sweetheart."

No way was Waxman going out. He put Linguina on his shoulders and went inside to the bedroom window where he could peek between the blinds. "Shit!" There were six cars in view and probably more farther down the street. Cops loved to show their force. Oh, well, he could play the game. He went to the back and turned on the karaoke machine, raising the volume loud enough to reach the street. "GO AWAY! THIS IS MY HOUSE. I'M NOT LEAVING!"

He crept back into the bedroom to see what effect his voice had created, and noted even more cop cars. He couldn't see Greta, so she must still have been on the side yard.

He went back to the screened porch and picked up the
microphone, blasting the volume, using a deep haunting
voice. "GO AWAY! YOU'RE NOT GONNA GET ME!"

The cops had the front entrance and side gate covered,
but he couldn't spot anybody way back in the woods. It
was broiling hot in the field, thick and buggy in the trees,
but they must be hiding there.

"WE DON'T WANT TO HURT YOU." *Hurt* was a
subjective word. If he opened the door to talk, he would be
carted away.

The dialogue continued. He got louder and spookier,
but they had nothing new to offer and he wasn't about to
give in. Linguina was tense and he became anxious about
the effect on her hearing. After a few more repetitions,
he turned off the karaoke machine and went back to the
bedroom. The cop cars were still there but he didn't see
any police. Where could they be? He peeked out the side
window. "Whoa!" A cop was crouched beside his car with
a rifle trained on the front door. The others must have been
hidden behind their vehicles taking aim in case he went
postal. Perhaps they did want to hurt him in an objective
sense. Greta must have told them he had a gun. It was an
antique shotgun on the wall, inherited from her side of the
family, without any shells, but she had probably left out the
details.

Now he was desperate, not for his own welfare, but
for Linguina's, the embarrassment of the situation and
poor prospects for her future. If they shot him or took
him to the hospital, she would be "rescued" and given
away to some kid who would never respect her or care for
her at the level she deserved. Even worse, she might be
euthanized. He couldn't let that happen.

The megaphone cop had shut down, and Waxman knew they were planning a move. He heard Greta's voice on the other side of the gate and tiptoed through the grass to hear what lies she was spreading.

She started to speak abnormally loud. "He's not coming out." It wasn't like Greta to go hysterical, so he wondered what was happening. The cops were muttering but he couldn't hear. Greta chimed up loud again. "I told you the only way in is through this gate or the front. Just break down the door like they do on TV."

It didn't make sense. Greta knew that the whole back of the yard was open. It was a long way around through the park and the woods, but the cops could swarm in from there.

It dawned on him. She knew he was listening and wanted him to make a break and never come back.

The banging started again, followed by the megaphone. "THIS IS YOUR LAST CHANCE BEFORE WE BREAK DOWN THE DOOR. COME OUT, SIR."

There wasn't any choice. He grabbed a plastic grocery bag and stuffed a handful of Linguina's outfits into it, along with the small sack of monkey biscuit. Through the open sliding door he heard splintering of the front doorframe. No time to take anything for himself or even to put on a shirt. He plunged through the screen door, holding Linguina's legs as he ran, barreling across the lawn, tearing between bushes into unknown territory. If he could make it to his lawyer, Greta would have to fight fair and he would get half the house back.

As he broke through the bushes at the end of the property, he panicked, realizing that Greta's words might have been a trick. He ducked as he ran, shielding Linguina

with his arms, expecting a shot to fell him at any moment
from cops stationed on either side. In fiction when guns
are involved, somebody gets shot. But this was real life, or
was it? The eternal question. He kept running and nothing
happened.

Halfway through the field, his energy started to sap.
He was light-headed and his body became heavy from the
waist down, his feet wanting to stick to the ground. But the
way was clear, and he dragged himself on.

Up ahead in the scrub were iguanas, maybe fifteen or
twenty. Huge varicolored monsters on the turf and in the
trees. They did not scatter as he approached, but remained
like fossils, their heads turned in his direction. He slowed,
ready to collapse from heat exhaustion, and devastated,
knowing that they wanted to stick their hemipenes into
Linguina's cloaca.

Linguina knew too. Her claws went deep as she
straightened her neck and rose up so that only her feet
were touching him.

Waxman choked out the words. "Do you want to . . .
go with them?" He swallowed hard as he pictured her neck
clamped by sturdy jaws, her slender form pinned under a
heavy, scaly body between powerful thighs.

She didn't answer, as always considerate of his
feelings, but the slant of her neck revealed the truth. His
stomach dropped roller-coaster style as he was struck by
the possibility that she might have been playing him all
along—for outfits . . . the Harley vest . . . to lure the wild
bunch before he was even aware of their existence. He
twisted his neck to stare into her eyes. They were glassy
with tears. No. Her spiritual love was sincere; nature had
become stronger. She was a queen among her species,

therefore, a pawn of natural selection. If he couldn't make the sacrifice of allowing her freedom, his *agape* had never been true. Deep down, he had known that this day would come.

At that moment the past and future became clear. Without Linguina he had no desire to keep the house. There was no reason to deprive Greta. Her need was similar to Linguina's. Greta was young and beautiful and none of this was her fault. He would go voluntarily into the hospital where he belonged, having caused her enough trouble through all their married years.

He stopped a few yards from the gang and recognized Mr. Mud at the forefront, the bright orange banner of lust waving under his chin. Linguina shifted her weight and dislodged her nails, as if she couldn't wait, her excitement growing in proportion to Waxman's disgust. Releasing her would expand the invasive population, but he couldn't think in broad scope when the happiness of his true love was at stake. Linguina and her progeny would certainly elevate the species.

With deepest regret he lifted her over his head and set her in front of him, dressed for courtship in all her Harley glory. Her feet touched ground and she sprinted toward the mud-colored brute without looking back. She passed by him, continuing on, and he followed.

Waxman was relieved to see that she would not perform sex in front of him. The reptilian army moved in formation toward the woods, Linguina graceful and proud next to King Mud, her skin becoming one with the underbrush. He followed the Harley vest with his eyes until it disappeared, monkey biscuit and tiny clothes dribbling from his hand.

Gators

It was a goddamned one-armed alligator put me over the line. After that I was looking for trouble. Carl and me had been married for two years, second marriage for both, and the situation was drastic—hateful most times—but I could tell he didn't realize there was anything better in the world. It made me feel bad that he never learned how to love—grew up with nothing but cruelty. I kept trying way too long to show him there was something else.

I was on my last straw when I suggested a road trip for Labor Day weekend—stupidly thinking that I could amuse him and wouldn't have to listen to his bitching about me and the vile universe on all my days off work. I figured at a motel he'd get that vacation feeling, lighten up, and stick me good, and I could get by for the few waking hours I had to see him the rest of the week.

We headed out to the Everglades for our little trip. Being recent transplants from Texas, we hadn't seen the natural wonders in Florida. Carl started griping by mid-afternoon about how I told him there were so many alligators and we couldn't find a fucking one. I didn't dare say that there would've been plenty if he hadn't taken two hours to read the paper and sit on the john. We could've made it before the usual thunderstorms and had time to take a tour. As it was, he didn't want to pay the bucks to ride the tram in the rain—even though the cars were covered. We were pretty much stuck with what we could see driving, billboards for Seminole gambling and airboats, and lots of soggy grassland under heavy black and blue-layered skies. True, it had a bleak, haunting kind of beauty.

Carl refused to put on the air conditioner because he said it sapped the power of the engine, so all day we suffocated. We could only crack the truck windows because of the rain. By late afternoon my back was soaked with sweat and I could smell my armpits. And, get this—he was smoking cigarettes. Like I said, I was plain stupid coming up with the idea—or maybe blinded by the fact that he had a nice piece of well-working equipment that seemed worth saving.

At that point, I started to wonder if I could make us swerve into a canal and end the suffering. I was studying the landscape, looking ahead for deep water, when I spotted a couple vehicles pulled off the road.

"Carl, look. I bet you they see gators."

"Fuckin' A," he bellowed.

He was driving twenty over the limit, as always—in a hurry to get to hell—but he nailed the brakes and managed to turn onto a gravel road that ran a few hundred yards off the side of a small lake. One car pulled out past us, but a couple and a little girl were still standing near the edge of the water.

It was only drizzling by then, and Carl pulled next to their pickup and shut off the ignition. My side of the truck was over a puddle about four inches deep. I opened the door and plodded through in my sandals, while Carl stood grimacing at the horizon, rubbing his dark unshaved chin.

We walked towards the people. The woman was brown-haired, wearing a loose print dress—the kind my grandma would've called a house-dress—and I felt how sweet and old-fashioned she was next to me in short-shorts and halter top, with my white blonde hair and black roots haystack style. The man was a wiry, muscular type in tight jeans and a white tee-shirt—tattoos on both biceps, like Carl, but arms half the size. He was bending down by some rocks a little farther along. The little girl, maybe four years old, and her mother were holding hands by the edge.

Carl boomed out "Hey, there," in his usual megaphone, overly-friendly voice, and the mother and child glanced up with a kind of mousy suspiciousness I sometimes felt in my own face. It was almost like they had him pegged instantly.

We stopped near them. The guy came walking over. He had his hands cupped together in front of him and motioned with his arms toward the water. I looked into the short water weeds and sticks and saw two small eyes and nose holes rising above the ripples a few yards out. It was a baby gator, maybe four feet long, judging by the closeness of his parts.

"There he is!" Carl yelled.

"Just you watch this," the guy said. He tossed something into the water in front of the nose and I caught the scrambling of tiny lizard legs just before the gator lurched and snapped him up. "They just love them lizards," the man said.

Carl started laughing "Ho, ho, ho," like it was the funniest thing he ever seen, and the guy joined in because he'd made such a big hit.

Us women looked at each other and kind of smiled

with our lips tight. The mother had her arm around the little girl's shoulder holding her against her hip. The girl squirmed away. "Daddy, can I help you catch another one?"

"Sure, darlin', come right over here." He led her towards the rocks and I saw the mother cast him a look as he went by. He laughed and took his daughter's hand.

The whole thing was plenty creepy, but Carl was still chuckling. It seemed like maybe he was having a good time for a change.

"Cannibals. Reptiles eating reptiles," he said. "Yup." He did that eh-eh-eh laugh in the back of his throat. It made me wince. He took my hand and leered toward my face. "It's a scrawny one, Virginia—not like a Texas gator—but I guess I have to say you weren't lying. Florida has one." He put his arm across my shoulder and leaned on me, still laughing at his own sense of humor. I widened my legs, to keep from falling over, and chuckled so he wouldn't demand to know what was the matter, then insist I spoiled the day by telling him.

We stood there watching the gator float in place hoping for another snack, and in a few minutes, the squeals of the little girl told us that it wouldn't be long. They came shuffling over slowly, the father bent, cupping his hands over the girl's.

"This is the last one now, okay, sweetheart?" the mother said as they stopped beside her. She was talking to the little girl. "We need to get home in time to make supper." From her voice it sounded like they'd been sacrificing lizards for a while.

The two flung the prey into the water. It fell short, but there was no place for the lizard to go. It floundered in the direction it was pointed, the only high ground, the gator's waiting snout. He snapped it up. This time he'd pushed farther out of the water and I saw that he was missing one of his limbs.

"Look, Carl, the gator only has one arm. I wonder what got him?"

"Probably a Texas gator," he said. "It figures, the one gator you find me is a cripple."

Carl had an answer for everything. "No," I said. "Why would one gator tear off another one's arm?"

"Leg. One big chomp without thinkin'. Probably got his leg in between his mother and some tasty tidbit—a small dog or kid. Life is cruel, babycakes—survival of the fittest." He stopped talking to light a cigarette. He waved it near my face to make his point. "You gotta protect yourself—be cruel first. That's why you got me—to do it for you." He gave me one of his grins with all the teeth showing.

"Oh, is *that* why?" I laughed, like it was a joke. Yeah, Carl would take care of his own all right—it was like having a mad dog at my side, never knowing when he might turn. He wouldn't hesitate to rip anybody's arm off, mine included, if it got in his way.

The mother called to her husband, "Can we get going, honey? I have fish to clean."

The guy didn't look up. "Good job," he said to his daughter. He reached down and gave her a pat on the butt. "Let's get another one."

It started to rain a little harder, thank God, and Carl motioned with his head towards the car and started walking. I looked at the woman still standing there. "Bye," I called.

She nodded at me, her face empty of life. "Goodbye,

sweetie." It was then she turned enough for me to see that the sleeve on the far side of the dress was empty, pinned up—her arm was gone. Jesus. I felt my eyes bulge. She couldn't have missed what I said. I burned through ten shades of red in a split second. I turned and sprinted to catch up with Carl.

He glanced at me. "What's your hurry, sugar? You ain't gonna melt. Think I'd leave without you?"

"Nope," I said. I swallowed and tried to lighten up. I didn't want to share what I saw with him.

He looked at me odd and I knew he wasn't fooled. "What's with you?"

"Hungry," I said.

"I told you, you should've had a ham sandwich before we left. You never listen to me. I won't be ready to eat for a couple more hours."

"I have to pee too. We passed a restaurant a quarter mile back."

He pointed across the road. "There's the bushes. I'm not stopping anywhere else till the motel."

We crossed the state and got a cheap room outside of Naples for the night. Carl ordered a pepperoni pizza from Domino's, no mushrooms like I wanted. The room was clean and the air and remote worked, but it was miles from the beach. We sat in bed and ate the pizza. I was trying to stick with the plan for having fun and I suggested we could get up early and drive to the beach to find shells.

"Fucking seashells? Forget it."

His volume warned me. I decided to drop it. I gave him all my pepperonis and finished up my piece. I had a murder book to curl up with. He found a football game on TV.

I was in the midst of the murder scene when Carl

started working his hands under the covers. It was half-time. He found my thigh and stroked inward. I read fast to get to the end of the chapter. He grabbed the book and flung it across the room onto the other bed.

"I'm trying to make love to you, and you have your nose stuck in a book. What's the problem? You gettin' it somewhere else and don't need it from me? Huh?"

I shook my head violently. His tone and volume had me scared. "No, for Christsakes." His face was an inch from mine. Rather than say anything else, I took his shoulders and pulled myself to him for a kiss. He was stiff, so I started sucking his lower lip and moving my tongue around. His body relaxed.

Pretty soon he yanked down the covers, pulled up my nighty and climbed on top. I couldn't feel him inside me—I was numb. Nothing new. I smelled his breath.

I moaned like he expected, and after a few long minutes of pumping and grabbing at my tits, he got that strained look on his face. "I love you to death," he rasped. "Love you to death." I felt him get rigid inside me, and a chill ran all the way from his cock to my head. He groaned deep and let himself down on my chest. "It's supernatural what you do to me, doll face, supernatural."

"Mmm."

He lit up a cigarette and puffed a few breaths in my face. "I couldn't live without you. Know that? You know that, don't you? You ever left me, I'd have to kill myself."

"No. Don't say that."

"Why? You thinking of leaving? I *would* kill myself. I would. And knowing me, I'd take you along." He rolled on his side laughing "eh-eh-eh" to himself. My arm was pinned, and for a second I panicked. I yanked it out from under him. He shifted and in seconds started snoring. Son of a bitch. He had me afraid to speak.

The woman and the gator came into my head, and I knew her life without having to live it, casual cruelty and then the injury that changed her whole future. I could land in her place easy, trapped with a kid, no job, and a bastard of a husband that thought he was God. Carl said he was God at least three times a week, trying to convince himself. I shuddered. More like the devil. He might take an arm first, or go straight for my soul, just a matter of time. He'd rather see me dead than gone.

There was no thought of a road trip the next weekend, so we both slept late that Saturday. By then, the fear and hatred in my heart had taken over my brain. I was frying eggs, the bathroom door was open, and Carl was on the toilet—his place of serious thinking—when he used the words that struck me with the juicy, seedy, sweet fantasy of getting rid of him.

"I ought to kill my brother-in-law," he yelled. The words were followed by grunts of pleasure and plunking noises I could hear from the kitchen.

"Uh, huh," I said to myself. Neon was flashing in my head, but I pretended to be half-hearing—as if that were possible—and splashed the eggs with bacon grease like he wanted them. I didn't say anything. He could build up rage on the sound of his own voice alone.

"The fuck went out on Labor Day and left Penny and the kids home. She didn't say anything about him drinkin', but I could hear it in her voice when I called last night. I can't keep ignoring this. I oughta get a flight over there and take ol' Raymond out."

"How's he doing after his knife wound?"

"Son of a bitch is finally back at work. I should just take him out. Penny and the kids would be fine with the insurance she'd get from GM."

"Oh?"

"Those slimy titty bars he hangs out in—like Babydoe's—I could just fly into Dallas, do him, and fly back. Nobody would think a thing unusual."

I heard the flush and then his continued pulling of toilet paper. He always flushed before he wiped. I knew if I went in there after him I would see streaky wads of paper still floating. He came striding into the kitchen with a towel wrapped around him, his gut hanging over. He seemed to rock back as he walked to keep from falling forward. He turned and poured his eighth cup of coffee, added milk, held it over the sink and stirred wildly. Half of it slopped over the sides of the cup. His face was mottled with red and he growled to himself.

I looked away. I remembered that at seventeen he had thrown his father out of the house—for beating his mother. He found out later they snuck around for years to see each other behind his back—they were that scared of him.

I knew going opposite whatever he said would push him. I pointed to the phone. "Calm down and call your sister. Her and the kids might want to keep Ray around."

"Yeah? Uh, uh. She's too nice. She'll give that son of a bitch chance after chance while he spends all their money on ass and booze. If anybody's gonna take advantage of somebody, it's gonna be me."

I handed him his plate of eggs and turned away to take my shower and let him spew. He picked up the paper again and started with how all the "assholes in the news" should be killed.

Before this, it didn't occur to me as an asset that he was always a hair's breath from violence. I'd tried for peace. I didn't want to know details about the trouble he'd been in before we met. I knew he'd been plunked in jail for violating a restraining order. He'd broken down a door too—I had that from his sister because she thought I should know. I figured he deserved another chance in life. He had a lousy childhood with the drunk old man and all. But now I realized how foolish I was to think that if I treated him nice enough—turned the other cheek—he would be nice back. Thought that was human nature. Wrong. Slap after slap to my dignity, until there was none of it left. I was a goddamned angelic savior for over a year and not a speck of it rubbed off. He took me for a sucker to use and abuse. It was a lesson I'd never forget, learned too late.

Something about the alligator incident made me know Carl's true capabilities, and I was fucking scared. That gator told me that a flight for Carl to Dallas was my only ticket out. It was a harsh thought, but Penny's husband wasn't God's gift either, and if Carl didn't get him, it was just a matter of time till some other motherfucker did.

At first I felt scared of the wicked thoughts in my heart. But after a few days, each time Carl hawked up a big gob and spit it out the car window or screamed at me because the elevator at the apartment complex was too slow, the idea became less sinful. He was always saying how he used to break guys' legs for a living, collecting, and he might decide to find some employment of that kind in Florida since the pay was so lousy for construction. Besides that, there was his drunk driving. If I could get him behind bars, it would be an asset to the whole state.

One morning he woke up and bit my nipple hard before I was even awake. "Ouch," I yelled. It drew blood and made my eyes fill up.

"The world's a hard place," he told me.

"You make it that way."

He laughed. "You lived your little pussy life long enough. It's time you find out what it's all about." He covered my mouth with his booze and cigarette breath, and I knew that was the day I'd make a call to his sister. He wasn't going to go away on his own.

Penny did mail-outs at home in the morning, so I called her from work. I could hear her stuffing envelopes while we talked. I asked about the kids and the dog. "So how's your husband?" I added. "Carl said he went back to work."

"Yeah. We're getting along much better. He's cut back on the drinking and brings home his paycheck. Doesn't go to the bar half as much."

"He's still going to that bar where he got hurt?"

"Oh, no, a new one, Cactus Jack's—no nude dancers, and it's only a couple miles from here, so he takes cab home if he needs to. He promised he wouldn't go back over to Babydoe's."

Done. Smooth. I didn't even have to ask any suspicious questions. "Yeah," I said. "He gets to the job in the morning. That's important."

"He only goes out Fridays and maybe one or two other days. I can handle that. I'm not complaining."

She was a sweetheart. I felt tears well in my eyes. "You're a saint, honey. I have to get back to work now—the truckers are coming in for their checks. Carl would like to hear from you one night soon. He worries."

I had all I needed to know—likely she'd wanted to tell somebody, anybody, and didn't care to stir Carl up and listen to all his godly orders. She wasn't complaining— goddamn. It was amazing that her and my husband were of the same blood. And, yeah, she was being taken advantage of—I could hear it. Now I had to tell Carl when and where to go without him realizing it was my plan.

That night I started to move him along. "I talked to your sister Penny this morning," I told him at the dinner table.

"Oh, yeah?" He was shoveling in chicken-fried steak, mashed potatoes with sawmill gravy, and corn, one of his favorite meals.

I realized I was eating with one arm behind my back, keeping it out of reach from any quick snaps. "She's a trooper," I said. "Wow."

"Huh?"

"I never heard of anybody with such a big heart. You told me she adopted Ray's son, right?

"Yeah. Unbelievable." He chewed a mouthful. "Him and Penny already had one kid, and he was fuckin' around on her. I'd've killed the motherfucker, if I'd known at the time. I was in Alaska—working on the pipeline. Penny kept it all from me till after the adoption." He shook his head and wiped the last gravy from his plate with a roll. "Lumps in the mashed potatoes, hon."

"She works hard too—all those jobs—and doesn't say a thing about him having boys' night out at some new bar whenever he wants. I couldn't handle it." I paused and took a drink of my beer to let the thought sink in. "He's a damn good-looking guy. Bet he has no trouble screwing around on her."

Carl looked up and wiped his mouth on his hand. "You mean now? Where'd you get that idea?"

I shrugged. "Just her tone. Shit. If anybody's going to heaven, she will."

"You think he's hot, don't you? I'll kill the son of a bitch. What new bar?"

"Cactus Jack's. I bet you he's doing it. She'd be the last to say anything. Why else would he stay out half the night?"

Carl threw his silverware on the plate. "I'll kill the bastard."

"I don't like to hear that stuff."

"It's the real world, and he's a fuckin' asshole. He needs to be fucked."

"I hate to hear a woman being beat down, thinking she's doing the right thing for the kids. 'Course, you never know what's the glue between two people."

"My sister's done the right thing all her life, and it's never gotten her anywhere." He was seething.

"She's one of a kind, a saint really." I tucked my hand under my leg—feeling protective of my arm—took a bite of fried steak, and chewed.

Carl rocked back on the legs of the chair. His eyes were focused up near the ceiling. "Hmm," he said. "Hmm."

"Don't think about getting involved. We have enough problems."

"You don't have a thing to do with this. It's family."

I gathered up the dishes and went to the sink feeling smug, even though I was a little freaked by the feeling that the plan might work. I was wiping the stove when the phone rang.

"Got it," Carl yelled.

It was Penny. She'd followed my suggestion to call. I could hear him trying to draw her out. He went on and on, and it didn't sound like he made any progress. By the time he slammed down the receiver, he had himself more angry at her than he was at her husband. He went raging into the bathroom and slammed the door shut. I was surprised the mirror didn't fall off.

I finished up in the kitchen and was watching *Wheel of Fortune* by the time he came out.

He sat down on the couch next to me and put his hand on my thigh, squeezed it. "You got some room on your Visa, don't you? How 'bout making me a reservation to Dallas? I'll pay you back. I need to talk to that asshole Raymond face to face."

I stared at the TV, trying to control my breathing. "He's not going to listen to you. He thinks you're a moron."

"A moron, huh? I think not. Make a reservation for me—"

I was shaking my head. "You can't go out there. What about work?"

"Do it—get me a flight out on Friday, back home Saturday."

"Not much of a visit."

He squinted and ran his tongue from cheek to cheek inside his mouth. "I'm just gonna talk to the motherfucker."

I'd never seen murder in anybody's eyes, but it was hard to miss. I took a deep, rattling breath. It was too goddamned easy—blood-curdling easy. I reminded myself it was for my own survival. I needed both goddamned arms.

That night I called for a reservation. I had to book two weeks in advance to get a decent fare. I'd saved up some Christmas money, so that way I didn't have to put the ticket on my charge. I could only hope nobody ripped Raymond before Carl got his chance. The guy that stuck Ray the first time was out on probation. It would be just my luck.

The days dragged. The hope that I would soon be free made Carl's behavior unbearable. I got myself a half-dozen detective novels and kept my nose stuck inside one when I could. I cooked the rest of the time, lots of his favorite foods, and pie, trying to keep his mouth full so I wouldn't have to listen to it. I also hoped to throw him off if he was the least bit suspicious of what I had in mind. It was tough to put on the act in bed, but he was in a hurry most of the time, and his ego made him blind, thinking that I could possibly still love him—and that he was smarter than everybody else.

Thursday morning, the day before Carl was supposed to leave, he walked into the bedroom before work. I smelled his coffee breath and kept my eyes shut. A tap came on my shoulder. "I don't know where that new bar is," he said. "What was it? Cactus Bob's? Near their place?"

"Jack's. Cactus Jack's. No problem. I'll get directions at work, online."

"Get the shortest route from the airport to Babydoe's and from there to the cactus place. He's probably lying to Penny, still going back to Doe's for the tits and ass."

I printed out the route during lunch. It was a little complicated. When I came in the door that evening, I handed Carl three pages of directions and maps. He flipped through them. "Write these on one sheet. I can't be shuffling this shit in the dark while I'm driving a rental around Arlington."

"Sure," I said. A pain in the ass to the end, I thought. I reminded myself it was almost over. I copied the directions on a legal sheet and added "Love ya, Your babycakes." Between his ego and my eagerness to please, I was sure he didn't suspect a thing. I couldn't wait to show him the real world when I gave him my ultimatum.

I got up in the morning and packed him a few clothes and set the bag by the door. I called to him in the bathroom. "Your ticket receipt is in the side pocket. Don't forget to give Penny my love." I knew he really hadn't told her about the visit.

He came out and took a hard look down my body. His eyes glinted and I could see satisfaction in the upturn of his lips, despite their being pressed together hard. There was some macho thing mixed in with the caretaking for his sister. In a twisted way, he was doing this for me too, proving how he could protect a poor, weak woman from men like himself.

I thought he was going to kiss me, so I brought on a coughing fit and waved him away. He thumped me on the back a few times, gave up, and went on out. He paused a second at the bottom of the steps, turned back, and grinned, showing all those white teeth. For a second, I thought he was reading my mind. Instead he said softly, "You're my right arm, doll-face." He went on.

I shivered. I watched his car all the way down the street. I was scared even though I was sure he had every intention of doing the deed, and I was betting on success. He was smarter and stronger than Ray, and had surprise on his side. Then I would hold the cards—with his record, a simple tip to the cops could put his ass in a sling.

I was tense all day at the office, wondering what he was thinking with that grin. I wondered if he'd packed his knife. When I got home, I went straight to his bureau. The boot knife was gone from the sock drawer. I pictured him splashed with blood, standing over Ray's body in a dark alley. I felt relieved. He was set up good.

I went to the grocery and got myself a six-pack, a bag of mesquite-grilled potato chips, and a pint of fudge royale ice cream. I rented three videos so I wouldn't have to think. On the way back, I cracked up laughing in the car, my emotions stretched between joy and hysteria. I couldn't stop worrying, but the thought of peace to come was delicious.

Carl was due home around noon on Saturday, and I realized I didn't want to be there. I got a few hours sleep and woke up early. I did his dirty laundry and packed all his clothes and personal stuff into garbage bags and set them just inside the door. I put his bicycle and tools there. I wrote a note on the legal pad and propped it against one of the bags, telling him to leave Fort Lauderdale and never come back—if he did, I'd turn him in. I said that I didn't care if we ever got a divorce, and he could take the stereo and TV—everything. I just wanted to be left alone.

I packed a bathing suit, a book, and my overnight stuff and drove down to Key Largo. The farther away I was when Carl read that note, the safer I'd feel.

I stayed at a little motel and read and swam most of Saturday, got a pizza with mushrooms, like Carl hated. On Sunday morning I went out by the pool and caught a few more rays before heading home. I stopped for a grouper sandwich on the drive back, to congratulate myself on how

well I was doing. I could barely eat it. Jesus, was I nervous.
I got home around four, pulled into the parking lot and
saw Carl's empty space. I sighed with relief. I looked up at
the apartment window. I'd move out for good, as soon as I
saved up enough. I unlocked the door and stepped inside.
The clothes and tools were gone. I shut the door behind
me, locked it, and set down my bag.

The toilet flushed. "Eh-eh-eh-eh."

I jumped. My chest turned to water.

The toilet paper rolled. Carl came swaggering out of
the bathroom. "Eh-eh-eh-eh," he laughed. The sound was
deafening.

"Where's your car?" I asked him. "What are you doing
here?"

"Car's around back. I wanted to surprise my
babycakes."

I looked around wildly. "Didn't you get my note?
You're supposed to be gone—I'm calling—" I moved
towards the phone.

He stepped in front of me. "I'm not going anywhere. I
love you. We're a team. Two of a kind."

"You didn't do it." I spat the words in his face, "You
chickened out."

He came closer. I could smell the cloud of alcohol
seeping from his skin and breath, a sick, fermented odor.
"Oh, I did it, babe, right behind Doe's. Stuck that seven-
inch blade below his rib cage and gave it a mighty twist. I
left that bastard in a puddle of blood the size Texas could
be proud of." He winked. "I let ol' Ray know why he was
gettin it too."

He took my hair and yanked me close against him.
He stuck his tongue in my mouth. I gagged but he kept

forcing it down my throat. Finally, he drew back and stared into my eyes. "I did some thinkin on the flight over," he said. "Penny'll remember telling you about the bars. Also, the directions are in your handwriting, hon. I rubbed off the prints against my stomach, balled up the sheet, and dropped it right between his legs. Cool, huh?" He licked his lower lip from one side to the other. "Oh, yeah, I found one of your hairs in my suitcase, so I put that in for extra measure."

My skin went to ice and I froze clear through.

"I was figuring it as insurance on our marriage—a nice little threat if I needed it to keep you around. A tip to the cops would be all it takes. Guess I saved myself a lot of trouble. Where I go, you go, baby-girl. Eh-eh-eh-eh. Together forever, sweetheart."

He grabbed my tee-shirt and twisted it tight around my chest. All the air wheezed out of my lungs, and he rubbed his palm across my nipples till they burned. He lifted my hand to his mouth, kissed it, and grinned with all his teeth showing. He slobbered kisses along my arm, while I stood limp. "Eh-eh."

Like the snap of a bone, his laugh shot chills up my spine and the sorry truth to my brain. I was the same as Carl, only he'd been desperate all his life. My damned arm would be second to go. I'd already handed Satan my soul.

M-F Dog

The broiling Key West sun was setting as Bob and I strolled the dog down Duval Street, the heat slapping our faces between buildings when there were no high walls or borders of bougainvillea for shade. It was a climate ripe for jock itch.

I had gotten the dog in hopes of attracting girls up at OSU who were looking for the wholesome, sensitive kind of guy who would care for a puppy. A broken leg had ruined that strategy, so I graduated and moved to the island in the summer with Bob. Both of us worked as waiters, hoping to write best-selling fiction. Writing a novel had been another plan for attracting women—or a woman—but I'd pretty much given up on that idea too.

The dog was no longer cuddly. However, he was beautiful, having reached an age when his muscles were well-developed, his purebred Doberman body sleek, and black eyes bright with mischief. His step was spirited with the adventure and cheer of an evening walk around town where everybody was his friend. He held his nose high, sniffing for cats and places to piss, his coat shining obsidian-black. Bob and I were less energetic. Sweat rimmed the necks of our t-shirts and rolled from between our shoulder blades to the waistbands of our shorts as we kept up his pace.

Key West was expensive, so we were renting a tiny, un-air-conditioned apartment made out of an old house that had been divided up. Bob had a girlfriend already—he always had one within days—a nice girl who spoiled him relentlessly. She waitressed at Louie's Backyard and had a small air-conditioned place with a pool where Bob usually stayed, rather than us taking turns between the bed and the couch. We would meet her at Louie's after work for a drink by the water.

I was unattached, as usual, alone. I'd always been weak in the knees around women, probably from needing somebody so badly, some connection to a female personality—sex—or even love. Normal women never liked me. I figured the dog would change that, but then I'd missed my window.

We decided to stop at the Iguana Cafe for a snack and a beer, where I could tie the dog in a shady spot on the sidewalk next to the table and feed him a bite of conch fritter or a shrimp tail now and then. He took things nice and slow from your hand. When we sat down, he cocked his head at Mr. Iggy in the cage behind us. Mr. Iggy turned his head and looked back—good attention skills for an iguana—and I was thinking the two might have some kind of inter-species understanding.

I looked at the cage and realized that this reptile had his own name tag hanging right there, unoriginal as it might be, and I still hadn't picked a name for a dog over a year old. But there was something pure and true about calling him "the dog," almost Hemingwayesque, and I decided to keep it that way.

We ordered a couple of beers and appetizer samplers

with the conch fritters and shrimp. I planned on a piece of key lime pie for dessert. We were killing time, or at least Bob was, waiting for his honey, while I was seriously looking for my honey, or sweetheart, or even a ball-buster, at this point. It had been so long since I'd been with a woman, I probably couldn't tell the difference. The dog was wagging and looking hopeful at each person who passed by, almost like he was trying to help, except he didn't discriminate between the girls and the boys. In Key West that's in no way unusual, but I was still holding out for female attention.

We drank our drafts and nodded at people who stopped to give the dog a pet. It was "Hemingway Days" week and we remarked on the huge number of white-bearded, beer-bellied, sweating, middle-aged men with their tolerant wives. There were a lot of compliments on the dog, and I said thanks, thanks, thanks, and felt proud that the scrawny pup I'd picked out at the Humane Society had grown into such a beauty. It said something for my powers of selection and care.

"Gawd damn, that's a motherfucking, good-looking dog." The words bellowed from the mouth of a tall, string bean of a guy in a backwards baseball cap. "A Gawd-damned, motherfucking, good looking dog." He stooped low and scratched behind the dog's ears.

"Thanks. He's a good dog."

"He is, sure is. He's a motherfucking, good-looking, son of a bitch, and don't let anybody tell you otherwise." He stared at me with defiance, like I would be one to argue.

"Yeah, he's a nice dog."

The guy took the dog by his collar and buried his face in the dog's neck, and I could feel my lips move toward forming a word, but I held back. He murmured into the fur, "Gawd damn, motherfucking, good looking, Gawd damn . . . . "

I looked at Bob and we agreed with our eyes—here was one drunk redneck that we'd have been better off to avoid. But it was too late. He straightened up and sat down on the empty chair next to the dog, his fingers working hard behind the ears.

The dog tilted his snout at me, tongue hanging out the side, and those shining black eyes got rounder. I swear we were thinking the same damned thing—grin and bear it.

A laugh came from the next table. There was a pretty brunette with a nose ring watching the drunk manhandle my dog. Her pupils were so large and dark, they might have been dilated—like most of the eyes in Key West on an evening—but it didn't matter. I was ready to fall in and drown. She was braless under a thin sleeveless tee shirt cut off just beneath her tits, some lovely tan ribs showing above the table. I already wanted her for a lifetime. I wondered how she could have sat down and ordered without my noticing. I searched behind her for the guy that must be on his way from the restroom or buying a pack of cigarettes, but there was nobody, and no other drink on the table.

I wasn't sure why she was laughing, but I looked at her and laughed along, like I was having a grand time sitting there with the drunk, instead of being fucking annoyed. She winked and toasted the air in my direction and I almost lost my breath as I took in her beautiful teeth, two perfect dimples, and innocent eyes sparkling brighter than all the Key West stars, even when you're out on a boat.

I felt a thump on the table and went back to where I

didn't want to be. The redneck was waving at the waitress behind the cash register who was either blind or ignoring him. "Gawd-damned, Gawd-dog. What's it take to get a beer around here?" He whacked the table top with a broad motion and Bob and I both grabbed our glasses.

"I hear Captain Tony has a good band tonight," Bob said. "Maybe you'd have better luck over there."

The guy looked at Bob and ice crystals formed between them, fast, despite the tropical air. "What's a problem, buddy? You mind me sitting at your table? I only come to say what a motherfucking, good-looking dog your friend here's got. You have a problem with that?"

My stomach clenched. Bob had been a linebacker at OSU, although he spent all his time on the bench. His hands were on his thighs and his posture had a spring-loaded quality that looked like trouble in the making. The dog had gotten bored and curled himself on the concrete, rhythmically licking his balls. I pointed at him and leaned closer to the drunk. "Know why he does that?"

The guy looked at me like I was the one cruising with the lights on dim.

I decided not to give the punch line. I shrugged. "Just wondering if you knew." I heard the girl sputter into her beer and start laughing. It sounded like some beer might have come through her nose, but I didn't look. The drunk gave me a nasty, sick look.

I took the dog's leash and tugged him up. "I'm going to take the dog around the corner for a piss," I said to Bob. I turned and stopped, hoping like hell the drunk would follow and I could lose him and loop back before the girl got away. With any luck she had food coming.

The drunk looked at me dumbly. "Come on," I said,

"He likes you. Let's take this motherfucker for a piss."

Once up, the dog pulled and I followed slowly. I was not about to take the guy by the hand, but finally he rose and stumbled after us. We walked around the block to a parking lot with a fringe of grass, and the dog raised his leg. I watched as he squirted the white parking stone, remembering when he used to squat and dribble, wishing he was still a pudgy and cute female attractant. The guy and I stood watching in silence while the dog finished and scratched the scrubby weeds. I motioned towards the Hog's Breath Saloon. "Hey, buddy, here's a few bucks. Get us a beer, would you?"

I pushed the money at him and he took it from my hand finally and bounced his head in a loose sort of yes. As soon as he had put one foot in front of the other, I took the dog and ran. His nails scraped as we took off across the sidewalk. When I got back to the table, Bob had finished up the appetizer plate. The other table was empty. All that in less than five minutes.

I was close to tears. "Where's the girl?" I asked Bob.

He looked to the side and around the cafe. "What girl?"

I didn't bother to answer. Sat down hard. Sweat was creating a prickly itch around my balls and I reached under the table and scratched. It was just like me, jumping up to save the day, when Bob could take care of himself perfectly well. A scuffle might have led to conversation. I'd let the woman of my dreams slip away. I gulped my beer. It was warm, as I deserved.

The sun had slunk below the buildings, and Bob suggested we walk the dog over to Mallory Dock. I agreed. The dog could sniff legs and enjoy all the petting while we celebrated the sunset by viewing braless women in t-shirts. Bob and I cut across the wide lot of tourists toward the silhouette of Will taking his nightly tightrope walk near the edge of the dock and some bruiser struggling in chains. Behind him the orange ball hung three-dimensional over the horizon. It was a sight, for sure, but I wondered how these guys could perform their acts night after steaming night. Some of them had been there for over twenty years—Will and the bagpipe player over thirty. The bagpiper had been wearing that heavy plaid skirt every night since the day I arrived. Poor sucker, but then he probably had a braless babe at home, like everybody did but me.

I had missed out on a real chance this time, since the girl had obviously enjoyed my sense of humor. Then it occurred to me—Key West was a small town, and she was dressed for a night out. There were a limited number of places where she could go, and I could rule out the gay bars and many others, considering her age and style. All I had to do was search. She was looking for company, and I had to find her before somebody else did.

From that thought on, I wanted to burrow through the crowd as quickly as possible and get back to the bars. I let the dog pick up speed, and he began pulling and winding around tourists. He was strong and I had to reel him in close to keep from leash-burning people's calves as he made his turns. Bob glanced at us with annoyance, but kept up and didn't comment. The dog whipped me around a card table set up for Tarot readings and nearly knocked it down. I grabbed a leg and steadied it, but the cards flew off. I bent to pick them up, trying to hold the dog with one hand and stack the cards on the asphalt with the other.

I glanced under the table at the pair of shorts above, some white, veined legs at my eye level. "Sorry, ma'am. So sorry. I hope I haven't mixed up your whole future."

I was wondering who would pay for this weird stuff anyway. I stood and stacked the cards in the center of the table. And there she was behind it—my fantasy princess, my nippled beauty, my only possibility—reading cards for a lady in a sailor hat.

"Your dog is psychic," she said.

My mind did a quick turnabout and snapped into spiritual acceptance before my face could reveal any doubt. I succumbed to instant belief in animal communication and Tarot cards. I felt my consciousness spread to embrace karma, crystal balls, numerology and astrology, charms, tea leaves, aromatherapy, acupuncture, and angels. Especially angels. I was a believer.

The dog began to buck and nearly took the table over. I was yanked forward, cursing my former god, and the crowd surged together between me and the two women, like the Dead Sea joining. I was yanked forward in the direction opposite of where I desperately wanted to go. I had given him too much leash, so that he was able to lever off the legs of the tourists and zigzag through the crowd. I cursed myself for the ridiculous idea of adopting a dog to attract female companionship.

I stepped on feet and walloped into hips. With a frantic dodge and grab, I maneuvered so not to trip an old tourist couple as they made their slow, hot progress across the dock. "Sorry, sorry. Excuse me, sorry." I kept the apologies going, as I got the dog under control, but tears were behind my eyes, in fear that my female vision of all physical and spiritual desire would again not be around when I got back.

Finally, there was a clearing in the crowd. I saw up
ahead that the dog had been making a streak for the
trained housecat act. Dominique had a black one poised to
jump through the fiery hoop and the dog was mesmerized.
We hadn't gone far, but the crowd was thick and I couldn't
see through to the girl. Bob was nowhere. I stood there
panting and the dog glanced at me, considering his next
move. I gave the leash several turns in my hand, so I had
his neck tight, and let go a few harsh words. I probably hurt
his feelings, but I didn't care. I started back toward where
the girl was.

"That's a mother-fucking, good looking dog."

I pivoted, still out of breath, expecting to see the drunk
and wanting to pop him. It was a different guy, a big six-
four, maybe 250-pound kind of guy with big shoulders and
long arms. He stooped and gave the dog some walloping
hard pats on the back. I stood baffled at what it was all
about, this dog again eliciting words of obscene praise.

A voice came from behind, and amazingly, my angel
stepped out of the crowd. "Hey, take it easy, buddy," she
yelled at the ape. "How would you like to be pounded on
the back like that?"

"I'd like it fine. Here, girlie, I'll bend down so you can
reach." He bent over, but the girl turned her back to him.

"The stars are lined up right tonight," she said, and
I took that to mean she felt lucky to see me again. She
laughed and her nose ring danced in the low rays of sun.

There were no stars yet, of course, and she could
have been sarcastically referring to the weird repeated
compliment on the dog, but I agreed.

She put out her closed fist over my hand. "You dropped

your keys under my table." They fell into my palm, and I slipped them into the deep pocket of my shorts without breaking eye contact. Bob and I had left the key under the mat at home, but I wanted a reason to be indebted to her.

"Thank you. Thanks." I gulped some air. "Hope I didn't mess up your business."

She shrugged. "It's all fate, one way or another. I'm finished for the night." She smiled.

I nodded, saturated by her huge liquid eyes. The big guy was staring at me over her shoulder, drunk and working up an attitude. He was standing on the dog's leash. Key West was fucked sometimes. I didn't want to waste more precious minutes, and I didn't want him whacking on my dog again either.

I looked around for something to distract him, but the square was a conglomeration of distractions so thick that there was nothing outstanding to remark on. I decided to go for honesty.

"Buddy, all I want to do right now is take this beautiful woman for a walk down the street and say the nicest things in the world I can and hope that she wants to get to know me. I never had a chance with a girl like this in my life."

I didn't dare turn to see the look on her face. I knew I'd given out way too much information and she'd realize that I was a putz and could never get a woman—all the rest of them knew something, so why should she waste her time?

The guy put his hands up flat on both sides of his head, like he was in a holdup, disarmed, and I saw that my words had magically hit on a male code that he could understand. "I need to take my dog with me." I pointed to the leash under his heavy boot, and he lifted it in an exaggerated move and stood there balancing. Just then the sun slipped beneath the water, and the nightly wave of applause rolled over the crowd. The guy bowed, taking credit for the beauty of the universe. I put my arm around the girl and turned, letting out a grateful breath, and we both followed the dog away from the dock, winding through inebriated tourists.

When we got back to her table, I folded up the legs and stuck it under my arm. She said she lived on Eden Street and took the leash from my other hand and walked the dog, who had finally worn down. I tried to set a slow pace beside her, dreading when she would say thank you at the doorstep, and it would all be over.

It was a short walk, very short. I propped the table against the porch rail and she passed me the leash and stood there, a one-second hesitation. I saw the word "Thanks" forming on her mouth in slow motion and her tongue touch her teeth, "Th--

"Can I buy you a beer at The Bull?" I said it too fast, like the classic dickhead I was.

She chewed her lip. "Okay."

I told her I was Lenny, and the beautiful name Alcira flowed from her lips.

As the night cooled and the smell of jasmine took over the atmosphere, we walked down the cracked sidewalks, stepping over roots and ducking under low-hanging trees and bushes together. We passed under a balcony, where the scent of weed mingled with the perfume of the flowers, and she said something about drugs in Key West, but I missed it. My ears had turned themselves off as my eyes became magnets to her lips, the plumpness, softness, the way they moved across her teeth when she spoke. I didn't even mind the nose ring.

We stopped outside The Bull and I looked for a place to tie the dog. Hard rock, the musty smell of old beer, and an overflow of bikers poured from the open doors and floor-to-ceiling windows. I pointed ahead, and we looked at each other and continued walking.

"Let's pass on that place. I've got stuff at home," I said, feeling brave in the drunken evening air. We strolled away from the crowd to where the sidewalks were cracked and the houses needed paint, my neighborhood. I walked Alcira across the dingy wooden porch and reached under the mat for my key, hoping she wouldn't notice, and wondering how long I could keep her there. I put the dog out back, brought her a beer and sat down next to her on the ugly green couch, roach-burned by former tenants, thinking I should have tossed a sheet over it.

She took a few sips from her bottle, then rose and slipped onto my lap like a cat. My arms went around her and my mouth to her throat. It was so easy. I heard her set the beer on the glass-topped end table.

"What else you got?" she asked.

"Uh, wine?"

"I hoped maybe you'd have a little X. I'm coming down."

"Sorry, no."

"Grass?"

"Sorry. But I don't mind if you smoke."

"Didn't bring any."

I was probably one of the few guys living in Key West without some sort of stash. It struck me that I wasn't her usual type, but I started kissing her neck again, ferocious yet tender, and after a few seconds she settled against me and began to tongue my ear.

Suddenly the dog became loud out in the yard, as if he knew I was finally getting some. Did he realize I was responsible for having him neutered? As my mouth went hard over Alcira's, the bastard hit a high-pitched yelp that cut like nails.

Then came the neighbor's guttural blast, almost as loud as the barking: "Fuck dis, mon! Shut dat motherfuckin dog up! Shut it the fuck up!" A door slammed.

There was silence for an instant and I felt something break, the spell of the night. I tried not to know it. The dog started up. Alcira drew back and looked me in the eye. I knew I should go out and bring in the dog, but I held on, praying for calm.

"That mother-fucking dog," I said.

We both began to laugh. We shook and howled and guffawed, holding each other by the shoulders, until all the loneliness of my lifetime tumbled down and disappeared between the cushions of the ugly couch, like small change. We couldn't stop snuffling and snorting, and the sounds of our laughter sent us into high abandon. She yanked off her shirt—as if it would help her breathe—her tits bursting out like sunset from under a cloud, her flushed nipples erect and magnetized toward my mouth. She draped herself over me and I dragged my lips over her chest, tasting her sweet saltiness. I began to believe that I did owe that mother-fucking dog something. I owed something somewhere.

Until the dog started barking again, I hadn't realized he had stopped. I buried my ears in Alcira's soft breasts and ignored him. He got louder and more irritating. I could picture him out there, his head and shoulders aimed at the door, ribs expanding and then his diaphragm punching out

the air, all his energy forced into his lungs and throat. His
ego was hurt. All night he'd been a star until I locked him
in the backyard.

There were footsteps on the porch. Somebody stopped
outside the screen door, on the other side of the wall next
to us.

"Shut dat mother-fucking dog up." It was almost loud
enough to rattle our beer bottles on the glass table.

I took Alcira's head in my hands and she steadied and
stayed quiet. The dog was woofing wildly out back. Alcira's
huge pupils shone. It was the two of us and the dog against
all the assholes in the world. I thought of letting the dog
in through the kitchen and out the front, but I was afraid I
would lose him. I stood up to face the fucker on the porch.

Something banged the doorframe. "Hey, mon, I know
you're in dere."

The latch wasn't even on. I stepped to the door and my
eyes stared straight into a bare tan torso, a washboard if
I'd ever seen one, then moved up huge shoulders to white
teeth in a smooth coffee face and long floating dreadlocks
nearly touching the porch roof.

"What can I do for you?" I said. I expected him to fling
open the door, stoop, and grab me by the neck.

"Look, mon, I'm tryin to get my little high on, and your
fuckin dog is—" He stopped, his eyes looking over my
head.

I turned to see Alcira pulling down her shirt behind
me and wondered if she'd shown a flash of tit. Her nipples
were big as peanuts under the thin cotton.

"Sorry," I said to the guy. I was about to use the same
pity line that had worked at the sunset, but I'd lost Mr.
Dread's attention. I wondered if a rough tap on his chest

would be helpful, but my hand didn't move.

Alcira was beside me at the screen. "You got a nice fat splif over there, mon?"

"Oh, yeah, I surely do, girlie. Surely, I do."

The next few seconds passed in a blur of shadow, a touch of breeze. Through my haze of disappointment I felt, more than saw, the door opening and Alcira passing by, the glint of nose ring as she turned and smiled, his arm going around her shoulder. Footsteps trickled down the porch, and I thought how light on his feet this Jamaican was for such a big man.

As I walked through the living room to let in the dog, Alcira's abandoned beer caught my eye and I picked it up and drained it. My companion for the night was worn out and dropped down on the terrazzo. I started to hate myself for not letting him in when he belted out that first bark ... or not nailing the Jamaican, a number of errors. The dog raised his head and nuzzled my hand, and I thought how lucky I was. He was a mother-fucking beauty, smart— and loyal. I was glad that I'd waited to name him until I appreciated the depth of his soul.

The Big O

My ass was tired of driving, and I welcomed the sight of the dented, mildewed trailers on the east side of Lake Okeechobee. Miles of trailer parks with single- and double-wides stretched down the road on the side by the lake, a few of them tidy, landscaped Florida retirement villages, but discarded refrigerators, and broken down cars were the landmarks of my interest. I needed the worst rubble-strewn lot and the cheapest tin can I could find.

Some months earlier, Merle and me had made a Sunday drive up from Miami to check out what we figured was an affordable lakeside resort. When he saw the layout, Merle said he'd rather pitch a tent in the Everglades, but I took note. It was a place where anybody could get lost, and I had it in the back of my head that I might need to do that soon.

It only took me a few months to stash some bucks and finance an old car. I'd managed to dodge the punch the night before and lock myself in the bathroom till Merle passed out. It wouldn't be the first time I'd left a man, far from it, and usually for less reason than I had now. My threats had lost all effect in the three years Merle and me'd been together, and I didn't want Chance toddling around a household like that.

I knew it would be rough. My dreams of making it as a fashion model were all dried up, and I lived for the nights, the high I could depend on with Merle and sweaty rough sex. Yeah, I'd miss em. They were my only relief from the boredom and bad luck that were all life ever had to offer. It took discipline to keep pushing Merle's appetite for my pussy out of my mind. He was hot shit. But I was determined. I had dreams for Chance—his name was no accident. He was the possibility for me to redeem my luckless life. I had to break out of my old habits before he was old enough to absorb his asshole father's anger into his sweet baby brain.

I was in my area, trashy trailer parks scratching bottom. Splintered wood, dead palm fronds, tarpaper, soggy insulation, shingles, and scrap metal waited for pickup, mounds of trash sprawling over the properties. Last year's hurricane litter would soon be this year's projectiles, crashing through windows, killing people. Not that I cared about people in general, just Chance. I reached behind me and stroked his soft little foot.

Hell, if it was my trash, I'd have just left it there too. That's the way I was, always dragging my ass, till teeth were in it. I couldn't say shit about anybody else. I fit right in.

I drove down the strip, reading names that would've been attractive if I seen them in the Yellow Pages. Lakeside Haven, Quiet Waters Retreat, Jenny's Big O Fish Camp, Water's Edge RV—sure there was water, a canal that flowed behind the trailers, but the 15-foot dike behind the canal, surrounding the lake like an Indian burial mound, didn't give a peek at Lake Okeechobee. The berm, as they called it, kept the lake from drowning thousands at every hurricane, like I heard happened in the twenties, when the

water flowed over farms. Even so, I wondered how all these
tin cans had made it through the last hurricane season. I
pictured them in a big blow, rolling and bouncing into each
other, corners smashed and contents banging around like
pebbles in a rock tumbler. I'd seen the wreckage of a trailer
park near the coast, a few homes untouched through sheer
luck, amid fifty or more smashed and resting on their sides,
soggy insulation hanging out in clumps. But here were
many survivors, thank god—cheap, crusty boxes, perfect
housing for an unemployed, dry-alcoholic single mother.

The Big O. I liked the nickname for Lake Okeechobee
for obvious reasons. No more big "O's" from Merle
though. Too bad.

Chance started to crank up with some whining in the
back seat. Not to blame him, he was barely a toddler, a year
old, and had been strapped in for hours. I glanced at my
watch. Pretty soon, time for him to nurse. I couldn't think
about that for long or I'd start to leak.

I was low on gas, food, and money, and needed a sweet
deal on the spot. No time for jawing with scraggly old farts
who expected to glare at my tits for free. I slowed to a crawl
and scanned the windows, seeing plenty "For Rent" signs,
all crappy places, but still above my finances.

The "Touch of Clapp"—Class—Trailer Park sign
caught my eye. I had to laugh. Local vandals had a sense of
humor.

Just past it was the office, a single-wide with rusty
awnings and ugly as the rest. For a person that reads men
way better than books, the scrawled white letters sprayed
on the glass sliding door, Merry Xmas, Dudes!—at least
six months old, or maybe a year and a half—told me this
was the right stop. Maybe the good-ole-boy manager was

the one with the sense of humor, and I didn't mind that either.

Nursing was handy in more ways than one. I pulled off the road beside a huge pile of trash, and unbuttoned my shirt—one, two. I'd hold back on button number three for now.

I stuck Chance on my hip and crunched across the gravel and dry sticks to the door. I could hear a baseball game on the TV. I put Chance's little hand inside my shirt, and he started to knead like a kitten. I chewed my lip, he was so cute.

I knocked. A dog barked, and a tall shadow flickered past the slit in the curtains. If this didn't turn out to be a straight, single, long-haired, druggie white boy, thirty to forty, I swore I'd turn lesbian.

The door opened. My sexuality was safe.

"Back off. Back off," he said and pulled a white-headed bulldog aside with his collar. The dog stopped barking and snuffled and snorted at my knees.

I tucked my chin a little so I could bat some lashes and look up at the dude with my big blue eyes. Chance was pawing my breast, exposing mucho skin, as if on cue. "I'm interested in a rental," I said.

The guy glanced at my tit. He was a young forty—or an old thirty-five. A hunk of blond hair fell over his eye, and the smell of beer, cigarettes, and slight B. O. drifted into my nose. I was in my element. He patted Chance on the head with a muscular arm tattooed to the wrist and smiled. The tattoo to tooth ratio wasn't looking good, but I couldn't afford to be choosy. Teeth were never a priority in the style I was accustomed to.

"Cute little sucker," he said and reached for Chance's

tiny hand, partway down my shirt. Mr. Tattoo's thumb
brushed the poking nipple, sending a chill down my chest,
and I knew the hook was set perfect.

"I've got a single-wide, fully-equipped with furniture
and kitchen utensils for $400 a month, including utilities.
It's got a leak in the plumbing so the bathroom floor is
rotted in the corner, but the rest is tight. I'd want two
months up front, one for the deposit. Need to have it
cleaned first, if you're interested."

"I need a place right now," I said and nodded toward
Chance. I licked my upper lip slowly. "I'm short on cash.
How about . . . if I do the cleaning myself?"

"How short are you?"

"I've got almost a month. Gotta keep a few bucks for
food till I find a job. Then I'll catch up."

"Not much work around here."

"I'm fast and cheap. I can always find something."
Chance started to whimper and stretch my shirt lower. I bit
my lip. "C'mon, pal. That rust bucket is sitting there empty.
I'll improve it for the next tenant."

The dude studied my tits, searching for his answer.

"Give me a chance." I felt my face light up in a smile.
I always got a good feeling when I used my baby's name.
Chance was all sweetness and innocence.

I pulled back my shoulders to make my chest stand out
proud. I winked.

"I can put you in there, if you give me $400 and clean
the place. When you get a job, I'll add on twenty-five bucks
a month until the deposit is paid."

"Three-hundred is all I've got. C'mon. You're not going
to rent that place this time of year. Everybody's left before
the mosquitoes could carry them away."

"You'll have to owe me the rest then. I'll give you a month and see how it goes."

I stuck out my hand. "Candy," I said. "Pleased to meet you."

"Jimmy," he said and shook on the deal. He pointed to the dog that had dropped down drooling. "Spike."

The trailer was the worst on the lot, but it had a little air-conditioner with a shredded La-Z-Boy under it, so Chance and me settled right in. I looked around at the cheap paneling and dirty carpet while I nursed him. I wouldn't be able to let him loose. Lucky I had his playpen and swing in the trunk. I just hoped there weren't bed bugs or other nasties to bite his sweet skin. I couldn't wait to get started on the cleaning. I could see a dead roach on the countertop from where I was sitting, and the bathroom was bound to be moldy as hell.

Life was exactly as I expected at the trailer park. A month later, having moved into Jimmy's place, I felt like I'd been there for years. I raised up from his sunken mattress and glanced in the mirror, then dropped back on the pillow. My eye was swollen and purple as a ripe eggplant. I looked down at Jimmy sleeping. With his mouth closed, tattoos covered by the sheet, and that blonde hair, he looked enough like an angel, so's I almost believed that he was sorry for the punch, even before he said so. He wasn't quite as cocky as Merle, because he just plain wasn't as cocky, but his cock was big enough. Leastwise, my asshole wasn't sore. And so far, he hadn't asked me for any money.

Jimmy yawned and dropped his arm across my chest. I was rock hard with Chance's breakfast and it hurt. "Fuck!" I pushed him away.

"Oh, sorry, darlin. Lemme kiss it and make it better."

He grabbed my arm and nuzzled into my left breast
before I could dodge him. The touch of his lips on my
nipple let down the flow and he laughed and tongued at
the warm spray as it wet his mustache. "I thought there was
only one hole," he said. "You've got yourself a sprinkler
head."

I tried to knee him away, but he was too close to get
any force behind it, and he had me pinned in a second and
clamped his face onto my nipple, slurping hard and cutting
with his few teeth.

"Stop it!" I yelled. "Get your rotten mouth off me!"

My voice woke Chance in his pen in the living room,
and he was whimpering. I tried to worm away, but Jimmy
had both my arms in control while he drained my sweet
milk. His erection pressed into my thigh, and all I could
think of was poor Chance, hungry and scared out in his
little crib, while Jimmy wheezed and sucked. Finally,
Jimmy broke off to breathe. I had his allergies to thank.

He swung over on top of me and stuck his cock in.
I was wet despite myself. He was busting to come, and
the strokes filled me up to a fine tightness. I beat him
by a few seconds with a groan and a hot gush, and he
pumped on out. His weight eased down on top of me, but
I pulled loose and made my escape. Chance was bawling
loud by this time. I headed to the shower to scrub off the
cigarettes and beer before I offered him what milk was left.
I could fill him up on baby cereal and strained bananas,
but I felt guilty as hell. I'd done wrong hooking up with
Jimmy in the first place. I wanted to bash out a few of his
teeth—which wouldn't leave him with any. I decided
right then that I was gonna pay him back for being such a

motherfucker.

Anger ate on me all week, until one morning while
I nursed Chance. I looked into his clear blue eyes and
caressed his powder-soft cheek and shiny hair, almost
transparent, like corn-silk, and thought, what am I doing?
He was all the motivation I needed to form a plan. Besides
teaching Jimmy a lesson, I needed money. With money, I
could forget the losers and have my chance—I smiled—to
be a good mother. I'd thought about getting a job, but that
wouldn't leave me any time for my boy. It was a vicious
cycle that only strong action could break.

I knew Jimmy ran a drug business locally and had his
stash in a heavy safe cemented in the floor of the Ted's
Shed behind the trailer. Running the park didn't bring in
enough to cover his daily habits, so he'd found a way to
skip the middle man and make a profit besides. I'd heard
him on the phone enough to know the code, and I walked
out to the shed with him a few times when he went to get
the money for his deals, but he always shut the door in my
face. I knew it was a keyed safe, because he kept that key
on his person, and hid it good when he slept. From the
looks of the nylon bag he'd bring out of the shed, there was
major cash-flow. He was only living in a dump because he
was used to it. He'd grab a gun from an end table drawer in
the living room. It was a .38, just like the one my uncle let
me shoot when I was a teen.

My eye had turned from ripe eggplant to green by then,
so I had to get moving before the evidence disappeared.
Besides that, after the milk incident, I could hardly fake
enough affection toward Jimmy to keep myself around. I
let him plug me, telling him I had a sore throat to stop his
slobbery kisses, but I couldn't keep it up much longer.

I couldn't think of any way to get the money, except by pure force. That was where Merle came in, dynamite on a half-inch fuse, bold as shit. He wasn't any kind of father material, but he didn't know it. He was bound to be frothed up like a rabid hyena already, since I snuck off and took Chance. That energy could be put to good use.

I remembered one day shortly after the little tyke was born. I was taking a putrid diaper off him, wiping pea-colored shit off his little red butt, and Merle came into the room drinking a beer. He just stood there with this look of wonder. I knew what he was feeling. I always had to bite my lower lip on the inside to keep from bursting with love. We both swore an oath that we'd eat baby-shit rather than let anything happen to our little guy. That choice never came up, but I knew I could use Merle's strong feelings to help Chance and me lose both those losers for good. I'd taken enough shit off men. Come to think, I'd taken abuse from every man I ever knew. There was nothing to recommend any of them—except their parts. I needed to get past that.

It took some guts to give Merle a ring. I was sweating a puddle in the payphone booth.

"Hi," I said.

"Where the fuck are you?" he hollered. "Where's my son?"

It was five-thirty and he had a good start on Happy Hour. He'd either quit his mechanic job or took off early to get a start on the weekend.

"We're fine, thanks."

"The cops are looking for you. It's illegal for you to take Chance and run off like that."

"I didn't think you'd notice."

"Fuck."

"Merle, listen, I'm really sorry. I made a big mistake. Is there any chance we can patch it up?" I smiled and hoped he could hear it in my voice. "For Chance's sake?"

"Come back and we'll talk."

"I can't. I'm up by Lake Okeechobee. The car's broke down and I'm broke. I can't get a job because there's nobody to watch Chance, and I owe the trailer park dude a bunch of money." I took a breath and made my voice sound pitiful. "He already beat me up once. You should see my eye. I'm scared."

"Oh, you're fucking him."

I heard something—like a beer bottle—hit the terrazzo floor and shatter. "Merle, sweetie, I just want you back. I want our little family together again."

He was cussing so loud I had to hold the phone away. I knew he considered me his property. I got goose-bumps.

Finally, there was a pause in obscenities. "I'm coming up there to take care of my son."

"I need you inside me, baby," I added, using a little gravel in my voice.

"Didn't I tell you I'd kill you, if you left me?"

"That wouldn't do either of us any good," I said.

He grumbled something, and then said he could get to the park around noon. I said I'd meet him at Butch's Fish Camp and Backyard Bar. Nobody knew me there, and I didn't want him driving into the Touch of Clapp so's his car could be identified.

That morning I seen on the weather report that a hurricane was headed our way, Beryl. She'd been off in the Gulf but switched course and now they expected her to cut straight across the state, anywhere between Clewiston and Okeechobee. The whole lake was in the red cone of warning, and I was glad I was getting out. I didn't want to be near the Big O, even though the berm was supposed to hold it.

I had to walk down to Butch's because I didn't want Merle to catch me in a lie right off about the car, so I put a cap on Chance and smeared the sunscreen thick on us both. It was sweltering outside and I knew the bar must be half a mile from The Clapp. Jimmy had drove to Lake Wales to pick up some trailer parts, or so he said. I figured he was making a drug run. He was always gone most of the day, taking Spike with him, and came back high, so it was good timing for the setup.

Merle walked into the bar right at noon. I saw him first. His mouth was hard and his eyes mean, but when he looked at me with Chance in a highchair, he couldn't hold back a grin. I felt a big one slide over my face too. He sure was pretty, with his square jaw clean-shaved and hard muscles bulging. It looked like the beer belly had tightened up some too. I had to get over all that.

He stared at Chance and me like we were the Madonna and Child.

"Hey, Merle."

His face hardened, but I knew I still had power over him. He moved close and stuck out his finger so Chance would grab it.

"What the fuck's the matter with you?"

"Nothing. I'm better now. That last punch you threw me loosened up my brain. I thought I could really leave you, you know."

He hung his head, and I figured that was as big a sorry as I was going to get, the motherfucker.

He sat down in the booth next to me, and I gave him
a kiss. He squeezed my thigh under the table hard enough
to remind me that it was time to get down to business.
I told him the story about Jimmy nursing off my tit and
pointed out the eye, which was a rainbow of colors by
then. I watched his neck get red. He considered himself a
protector of women and children, even though he was just
as likely to break my nose as look at me. He couldn't wait
to go over there and rip Jimmy a new asshole.

I waited to spring the drug money idea on him, since it
involved murder. We ate some cheeseburgers and he drank
some beers. Didn't take long to loosen him up.

"You know, Merle, that asswipe deals drugs on the
side—to high school kids. He's got a safe in his shed just
full of money. I sure worry about Chance when he's a
teen, with those kinds of guys around. He's got no morals
whatsoever."

Merle looked over at Chance and I could see he was
thinking. His brain was hard and soft at the same time.

"It would serve him right if somebody got a hold of
that stash," I told him. "Jimmy's no asset to the world."

"You got any brilliant ideas?"

I shook my head. "Not sure. He keeps the key to the
safe on a chain around his neck. I think he even wears it in
the shower."

"He don't trust nobody."

We had another beer and then the weather report came
on the TV at the bar. Beryl was strengthening and still
moving in our direction. It was only a Category One so far,
but all mobile homes were on mandatory evacuation by
Sunday night.

"Better start packing up, all you guys in the double-wides," the bartender hollered. "Beer cans are gonna roll!"

There was excitement in the air, even though hurricane prep was a major pain in the ass. "Hmm," I said. "I wonder what asshole Jimmy does for a hurricane."

Chance started to fuss. He had a big mess of wet crackers crumbled on his tray, but I knew what he wanted. "Let's go out in the truck and crank up the AC. I can tell you my idea while I feed Chance."

It was a simple plan. We'd knock out Jimmy in his trailer and leave him for the hurricane. He was a dumb enough fuck that nobody would question his decision to stay. We'd whack him with a piece of wood so when the trailer got tossed around it would be a natural injury, like a shelf or a table got him. If that seemed unlikely to happen, we'd pull his body out on the ground after dark so it looked like he got hit by flying debris.

"I heard that some guy died last year when he stepped outside for a smoke and a tree limb hit him. Probably happens all the time."

"I bet his wife wouldn't let him smoke in the house," Merle said. "Sounds like something you'd make me do." He laughed. Then he stopped. "You're talking murder, Candy. You know that."

"So, what? He's a scumbag. Without him, the world will be a better place. I bet you already killed somebody in your life for less reason."

He didn't answer, so I figured it for a yes.

I knew I was a pretty picture feeding Chance with my shirt unbuttoned and my tits loose and sweaty. I gave Merle a slow smile and put his hand part on Chance's cheek and part into my cleavage. "We need a fresh start and there's nothing like a pile of money to help us get along." I

stretched my neck to give him a long kiss and tongued and
nipped his throat until I figured the bargain was sealed.
There were people in the world only a cunt-hair away from
murder. You just had to know how to spot em. It was my
job to get Merle and Jimmy together.

"There shouldn't be any suspicions," I said. "I don't
have any friends here, and it would make sense if I never
came back after the hurricane."

"What about the time of death?"

"I don't think they'd know that close, if you knock him
off late Sunday."

"This is my job?"

"You're the man, darlin. We'll turn the AC down low so
he stays cold until the electricity cuts off—if it does."

"We can't stay in there when the hurricane comes."

"So, we put the money in a suitcase and head to the
shelter. It's easy."

We set the time for the deed at 9 pm, so it would be
dark, and most everybody else would be gone, but we'd
have plenty of time to get the money and get out before
Mother Nature dealt us her blow. In my mind, it would be
enough time for me to shoot Merle besides.

Merle went off to a motel since he couldn't be seen at
The Clapp. I walked home to sweat it out with Jimmy and
set him up for Merle's arrival.

"He's a maniac, I'm telling you. If you got a gun, you
better get it ready so you can scare him off. I don't know
how he found me, but my best friend called this morning.
He might already be headed this way."

"With a hurricane coming?"

I shrugged. "He's a madman."

"Maybe you oughta just leave. I'm not in any of this."

"He's out for you too."

"Christsakes, why? How could he know anything about me?"

"I bet he got a P.I. That's all I can think."

"Cock-sucking motherfucker."

Sunday morning people were cranking down their awnings and clearing out. By mid-afternoon there was a solid river of traffic going north and about half that flow headed south. I guess it depended on where the friends and relatives lived. Since Beryl could change course, especially when she made landfall, neither direction was safe because you might be driving straight into her path. You run out of gas and the stations are shut down, you're pretty well fucked.

I would have liked to got moving, though. I was nervous for Chance, knowing we had to stay late, but the shelter was only a few miles away in the high school and we were still only looking at a Cat One. I went ahead and put Chance's porta-crib and swing in the trunk and packed the clothes and some bedding for me.

Jimmy said he had lots of hurricane prep to do at the park, checking the augers for the tie-downs, moving porch furniture and other junk. He was working on a cooler of beer at the same time, so I didn't have to worry that he'd be headed out early. Everything was going just right. I used dishwashing gloves when I got the bullets out of his .38, so only his prints would be on there. I waited to make supper late, cooked Jimmy a few hotdogs. I figured I'd put a couch pillow over the gun barrel the way they do on *The Sopranos* when I killed Merle, just in case there were still cops around. Under the sound of the wind whipping and rain drumming, the crack of the shot could be anything.

It would be easy to make it look like Jimmy shot Merle and then let the hurricane take care of the rest of the evidence. I'd leave a small amount of money in the safe, and nobody would know anything was missing. Later, when the cops tracked down where Merle came from, they'd figure Jimmy plugged him in a fight over me. It wouldn't be no surprise to anybody, and I'd squeeze out a few tears when they told me.

I had Chance asleep in his stroller in the back bedroom, and it was eight-thirty when Jimmy stuffed the last half of his third hotdog into his mouth and pointed his beer bottle toward the road. "I think your friend decided to hunker down at home, just like I thought."

"No friend of mine. Might be all the hurricane traffic slowed him down. You got that gun handy in case, don't you?"

"Always got it handy, babe." He cocked his head toward an end table, and I knew the gun was still in the drawer where I'd found it and put it back that afternoon. He took his beer, rousted Spike off the couch, and punched on the remote. "I don't want to leave Spike and go to that disgusting shelter until I have to. Maybe you should leave with the kid now."

"I'd rather wait for you," I said, but I was sure starting to worry about the storm. The flow of traffic outside had dwindled to almost nothing, so every time I saw headlights my heart started to pound. I wanted to get it done, but I didn't. I knew Jimmy was no match for Merle, especially if he was pointing an empty gun, but chance was always unpredictable. I smiled.

The wind was loud through the trees, and I was almost gonna take Jimmy's suggestion. Let Merle take care of him and just get away. Finally, lights swung past the window. The sound of tires pulling off the road set me on the edge of my chair. I didn't need to fake being nervous. "That's him. That's Merle. I knew it."

Jimmy sat up and motioned me to stay in my seat. The engine was shut off, and footsteps crunched on the drive. He'd parked behind my trailer, like I'd told him. I grabbed Spike and held him.

The knock was soft, just like I'd said to do.

Jimmy slid open the drawer and took out the gun. He walked to the door and opened it a crack.

"You got something of mine in there. You know what I mean?"

Jimmy pulled up the gun, ready to show it to Merle through the crack. "You get off my property while you still can."

Merle ripped the door out of Jimmy's hand and threw himself into the room, the door banging closed behind him with the wind. Jimmy pulled the trigger, once, twice. His face drained and he flung the gun toward Merle's head. There was a flash of a two-by-four and Merle had him on the floor, out cold, his forehead bloody. I was sitting on Spike, who was barking his head off.

"Whack him again," I yelled. "Make sure."

Merle bent over and gave him a couple more hard ones in the same spot. The gun was on the floor next to me and I slid it under the sofa with my foot.

Chance started to whimper in the bedroom. I shoved Spike into the bathroom and slammed the door. "Key's in his jeans' pocket. You get it, and I'll get Chance. Meet you in the shed."

He picked up the bloody two-by-four. "I better put this

in the truck so we can toss it."

"Good idea," I said. I was thinking that I had to remember to bring the board back.

He went outside, and I took the gun into the bedroom. I had to change Chance's diaper, put on the plastic gloves, and reload the bullets. When I brought Chance out to the living room, the body was laying there just the same, but Merle must've got the key off him and went to the shed. It wasn't a pretty sight in front of me, the dead body and ugly green shag carpet soaking up blood. I put Chance on the couch and hid the gun behind the pillow. Chance reached for the shiny gun, but I pulled him away in time. I didn't want to mix up any baby fingerprints with Jimmy's.

The trailer wobbled and squeaked in its tie downs. Once Merle got back into the trailer there'd be no reason to poke around, just shoot and run. I was spooked by the sound of the wind and the bad reputation of the metal coffins.

Merle was taking too long. I wasn't sure whether it was safer to carry Chance with me or leave him inside, but I stuck him on my hip and tore out of there. It was wild outside, garbage cans already rolling around, branches whipping by. I shielded Chance with my arm and ran to the shed. The door was closed and for a second I thought Merle had snatched the money and left me, but when I yanked it open, he was zipping the overnight bag.

"You didn't take it all, did you?"

"No, I left a pack of twenties and two ziplocks full of crack, so everything looks normal. No sense trucking that shit around anyway." He hefted the case, weighing it in his hand. "I don't know how much this is, but several of these packs are hundreds."

"Give me a look."

He unzipped the top and picked out a pack of hundreds, flipping the bills close to my face. There was only one dim light bulb in the shed, but I could see more packs of money in the bag.

"You were right," Merle said. His eyes were big with excitement. "We're rich." He grabbed my hand as I reached toward the bag. "Why the gloves?"

"I been doing some cleaning up."

"Wiped my prints off the door?"

I nodded. "Okay, let's put the key back around Jimmy's neck. It's getting crazy outside." I was too freaked to be happy. I still had to commit murder and escape the storm with my baby.

I followed Merle back into the trailer and put Chance in the corner of the couch. Merle knelt down by Jimmy with the key, wiping it on his shirt, putting it back in Jimmy's pocket. I picked up the pillow and the gun behind it.

Merle was shaking his head. "What if the hurricane doesn't break this sucker up? The cops'll know it's murder. Moving this asshole outside won't work either because the blood's in here."

"I never thought of that," I said. I had the gun pointed at him from behind the pillow. "Jeez, what should we do?"

I didn't wait for an answer, just squeezed the trigger. I hadn't done much shooting before, but being close, I hit him in the chest, and he fell backward, dropping the bag, oozing red down the front of his shirt. Chance was screaming bloody murder and Spike was barking like a maniac, but I stood over Merle and gave him one more to the head to make sure. Clumps of gray jellyfish stuff spattered onto the wall. It hit me then, what I'd done. Chance was still bawling hard, but I had to race into the bathroom past the dog to puke.

I splashed my face and ran back to Chance just in time before he could fall off the couch into the mess of Merle and Jimmy. I grabbed him and hugged him tight. "Don't cry, sweetie," I told him. He was scared by all the noise, and maybe the scenery. I wished I could explain how it was all the best for him in the long run.

Spike was sniffing around Jimmy, and I felt real bad about that. He was really a good dog, but there was nothing to do but shoo him out the door. He'd have to find a safe place to hide while Beryl passed over.

I put the gun in Jimmy's hand and closed his fingers. If the trailer went, everything would be tossed around messing up the evidence. Even if it didn't, it would seem like Jimmy revived long enough to shoot Merle—the way it happens in the movies. There was only a few minutes between their times of death. I doubted I'd be a suspect, since I didn't have a motive to kill either of them—except that they were men. The cops wouldn't think of that one. Merle, on the other hand, was well known for his temper, and Jimmy was a drug dealer with a gun.

Chance wailed, rain pounded the aluminum roof, and the trailer creaked and shuddered. There was a snap and crackle in the roar, like Rice Krispies, that I recognized as all the tiny dead branches popping off trees from the force of a gust. I'd seen and heard that before, in my last hurricane experience. Those heaps of rubble from last year must've been scattering too, all projectiles looking for a head to smash. The lights went out. I set Chance back on the couch and felt my way outside to the pickup for the bloody two-by-four.

When I ran back inside to toss it on the floor, Chance was so quiet, I thought he'd fallen off the couch and knocked himself out. I started to panic, but I felt for him and there he was. I prayed he wasn't traumatized. I held him to my chest, grabbed the bag of cash, and dashed to the car.

I held my breath as I drove, dodging branches and trash cans, all kinds of unidentified debris. Now, according to the radio, Beryl was up to a Cat Two, and the outer bands were already hitting the Big O. The berm was expected to hold, but there could be small breaks and minor flooding.

I laughed when I saw the high school with lights still on. "We made it, baby love. You're my lucky Chance!" I parked in an area blocked from the wind by buildings and took a deep breath. God finally sent good fortune flowing my way. He helped those that helped themselves.

There was nobody outside, and I couldn't resist a peek at the money. I hoisted the bag onto the seat. It was heavy. With all those hundreds, there should be enough to cover years of cheap living until Chance started school. One thing I knew was how to live cheap. I wouldn't skimp on Chance though. I'd buy him all the fancy educational toys. He would love the one where you touch an animal, like a bear, and he growls and says "bear."

I laughed, just thinking about the fun we'd have, and unzipped the bag and pulled out a pack of bills. I flipped through them. A hundred on top—but the rest was ones! I reached back into the bag for more, only found two, and they were all singles. I dug down. Old newspaper and cans of beer from the floor of Merle's truck. My head boiled with rage and I thought the top might fly off. "Damn you,

you cocksucker!" I screamed out loud to Merle.

Chance started to cry and I had to shut up and swallow it down, but I never wanted to kill somebody so much in my life. It was frustrating, since fucking Merle was already dead.

I dropped the packs of ones and turned the key. I had to go back. I pulled out from between the buildings and into the wind. Big chunks of wood and metal, were flying around now, and that was just the stuff I could see in the headlights. I tromped the gas and turned onto the road. Something slammed into the side window and flew off. The glass broke into tiny beads that splattered inside the car. Rain poured in. Chance screamed like I'd never heard him before. I looked close, but couldn't see any blood. It was pure terror. I let out an angry roar at the wind and pulled back between the buildings. I couldn't risk the drive. If something happened to Chance, all the money in the world would be worthless to me. I pulled back into the sheltered spot. I doubted I could return for the money after the storm. I'd be seen and become a suspect for sure.

I couldn't stop my tears as I bundled Chance into a blanket and carried him inside the building. I didn't even have enough money to rent a sleazy trailer. With my usual luck, I was in the same damn place where I started, except for I'd learned a lot about murder. I'd took right to it.

Lights were bright inside. The auditorium was packed, mostly old people and Spanish-speaking families. I found a cot, sat down, and adjusted my shirt to settle Chance with a nipple, calming him and trying to stop my own sniffling. I wasn't showing much tit, but I felt eyes on my chest.

I glanced across the room. There was a looker all right, big guy in a cowboy hat, legs spread, sitting on a folding lounge chair, shuffling a deck of cards. He looked free and open to suggestions. I felt a juicy twinge. The Big O that I hadn't had for a while came into my mind and slid over me. Those jeans were snug and I liked the boots. I was too tired to think much farther.

I let my head hang, watching Chance, his feathery lashes on his cheeks, suckling like an angel. My plan had failed, but at least his father was out of the picture—no more worry about violent assholes as his role models. I tilted my head up with one last bit of energy and winked at the cowboy.

As I relaxed and drifted off, I saw the Big O rushing over the berm and felt the cold water pour over us. It was like being caught under a wave, but I knew I was dreaming, so I didn't struggle. My luck was changing. I just had to hold my breath till the sun came out.

West End

Kyle switched hands on the tiller and gave Regina his used toothpick. She looked at the frayed end and flipped the pick into the Atlantic.

"Regina, you know we only have half a pack left. I wanted you to put that back in the galley to save for tomorrow."

"Sorry, Kyle, I thought it was finished. I can do without my share."

"One end was perfectly good. Just ask if you're not sure. Always ask. Remember that."

He turned his head the other way and she saluted. He looked so distinguished with his graying hair curling from under his hat, but he never lightened up on her education. They had been sailing the *Spring Fling* together for the last six years of their marriage. Kyle was a sailor above all else, even when the idea of owning a boat was just a twinkle in his eye.

"Nice turn of the bilge," he'd said to her the first time they slept together, when she was just nineteen, nearly twenty years in the past. At the time she didn't know he was comparing the shape of her buttocks to the hull of a sailboat.

He turned back to face her. "Do me a favor. Go down

into the cabin." He looked off to port.

"And do what?"

"Go down and I'll tell you when you get there."

She felt a retort like backwash in her throat but swallowed it. She turned to step down the companionway steps.

"Regina!"

"What?"

"Oh, I thought you were going to walk down forward instead of backward," he said.

"Don't you think I know anything?"

He didn't answer, staring off into the horizon again.

"Okay. I'm waiting. Kyle?"

"Go into the forward starboard locker on the second shelf toward mid-ships."

"And?"

"Get the little black leather case and find my fingernail clippers."

"Why didn't you just ask for the clippers? I know where you keep them."

No answer.

She didn't expect one. She took the clippers up and pressed them into his hand.

"Now take the tiller. Keep the compass on 90 degrees."

"Gotcha, skipper."

Regina took the smooth varnished tiller and held it gently with two fingers as Kyle had shown her again and again. She shifted her eyes from the compass to the top of the mast to check the wind vain. They were sailing on a run, straight downwind, with the jib to port and the main to starboard. It was going to be tricky to keep the boat on course and the sails filled. She didn't want to jibe. Even in these light conditions, Kyle would have a fit. The Pearson 42' was their only child.

Kyle put his head down and began working on his nail.

Regina was sailing well, keeping the course, barely moving the tiller. She'd found the groove.

Kyle said he needed to go down to take off his foul weather gear and get into some lighter clothes.

"Fine, honey," she said. "I've got it."

He stepped below and she filled herself with fresh salty air. She looked at the small islands in the distance, Carter Cays. They only had three miles to go until they could anchor for the night and make a nice conch chowder for dinner. Conch. Conch had become her favorite seafood. She remembered the conch fritters she'd had at the Star Bar in West End a few days before.

She envisioned of one of the locals, Rodney. She had danced three times with him. Ooh, the sway of his young hips, the way he smoothed her hair behind her ear. He said he liked long blonde hair. He was probably fifteen years younger than she was. Kyle was fifteen years older. That was balance, she thought. Just like the sails. If the sails are balanced, the slot is just right for maximum speed and stability. Sailing, that's what she should be thinking about.

The jib began to flutter. "Starboard!" Kyle said. He always caught the least sound, didn't even look up.

She'd already turned slightly to starboard, but as always, she jumped at his order and turned some more. It was too much. The wind caught the backside of the main, and before she could correct her course, banged the boom across to the other side. The noise sent lightening zinging through her brain.

"Fuck. God damn, Regina. You trying to tear the

rigging off the fucking boat. Can't I count on you to do anything for one second? Jesus Christ!"

She didn't answer. It was true, she'd let her mind wander and her hand followed. She needed practice. But maybe she didn't want any. She looked at the mast. Luckily no harm was done. Kyle went forward to inspect.

The long day became longer when Kyle felt it necessary to re-anchor three times at Carter Cays. He refused to buy an electric winch, being a purist in every sense. He refused anything to make sailing easier and only used the engine for docking, anchoring, and emergency. They'd sit for days if the wind died or tack for a week with the wind tight on the nose. He even anchored and picked up under sail, if possible.

Today, thank God, it wasn't possible in the small space between the island and the shoal. Kyle pulled in the anchor from the bow while Regina worked the tiller and throttle.

"Starboard, more, more!" Kyle screamed.

"Starboard!" She repeated his order as instructed. She had pushed the tiller immediately, but the boat never responded fast enough for Kyle. Soon she'd gone too far.

"Port! Port!"

"Port!"

"Neutral! Neutral!"

"Neutral!" she yelled.

She went through it at every stop, each spring, when Kyle decided it was time for a couple of relaxing months in the Bahamas. True, she loved the water and exploring the small cays and snorkeling across the shallows to find conch. She could swim with the exotic fish and nosey barracudas all day, but Kyle's anal attitude never ceased to make her nervous and upset.

He dropped the main and told her to get the sail cover, although she was already bringing it up from below. She tied the cover over his neatly rolled sail, exactly as he had instructed her over the years, shifting and straightening it until it was perfect and she was dripping with sweat.

"Sit down," Kyle said when she'd finished. He was sipping a gin and tonic. He motioned her into the cockpit.

She thought of having a drink herself, but decided to wait until after his lecture. He wouldn't think she was attentive enough.

"Do you know why you jibed today?" he asked.

"Yes, I do," she answered.

"Then tell me."

She gave a long and tedious description of how she'd turned too far and the wind had gotten behind the sail, then waited through his repetition of everything she already knew. Her mind floated back to the Star Bar. She was caught up in a warm breeze of memory and feeling, swaying next to Rodney, although she had never touched him.

"I only tell you this and go over everything so carefully because I want you to be the best sailor you can be. Understand?"

"Yes, I do," she said.

He squeezed her shoulder and kissed her. "Now cook us one of your delicious dinners. And be careful not to use more than one paper towel. We only have three rolls left."

Regina knew they could buy supplies on Green Turtle in a couple more days, but no way would Kyle pay the double prices of the Bahamas.

She stepped down into the galley and started peeling

the potatoes for conch chowder. Her mind went right back
to the warm place inside itself, the dim, paneled interior
of the Star Bar. The juke box was playing and Rodney was
touching her hair. It was the only detail she needed.

Kyle fell asleep early that night. Regina was grateful. He
was as demanding a lover as a captain.

She sat on deck. The anger begin to seethe in her
stomach, hotter than the Tabasco sauce in the chowder.
She wondered how many more times they would have to
make this trip. She'd thought last year was the end. Kyle's
epileptic seizures had recurred after years of no incidents.

"We could fly over and rent a luxury suite at the Green
Turtle Club," Regina had suggested. "Take it easy for a
change."

"Over my dead body," Kyle had shouted. "I'm not
going to sit in a hotel room and be waited on." The volume
of his voice convinced her, although she hadn't noticed his
opposition to being waited on.

Having built up his business, Kyle could afford to
hire another computer engineer and cut his own working
hours. The doctor put him on new medication, and Kyle
had himself under control again. He insisted the sailing
calmed him and made him forget the stress of work, the
snarls of traffic, and his brother the alcoholic, who was
always in need of money.

She knew she should sleep because Kyle would be
up at first light, ready to put the outboard on the dinghy.
They planned to head to the reef where they'd found
conch a few years before. But she couldn't settle down and
quench the singeing resentment in her throat. She stepped
down into the galley to get a toothpick. At least she could
dislodge an annoying bit from between her teeth.

She opened the box and took one pick out. The box was nearly full. Kyle had lied in order to make her feel guilty. A smug feeling came over her. She shook half of the toothpicks into her hand, and put the box back. She went up on deck and looked at the moon, a pearl sliver, and flung the toothpicks away, out into the water. She heard the lightest shower as they hit. It was too dark to see, but she imagined them headed away like a little flotilla toward freedom.

Kyle wouldn't be able to comment. There was still half a box left like he'd said.

After that she dozed right off, facing the sky on a seat cushion with a beach towel pulled over her. She was looking at the Pleides, Kyle's favorite constellation, imagining Rodney's lips on her neck.

In the morning she awoke full of lightness and energy. She knew they'd be spending a lazy day exploring in the dinghy and snorkeling the shallows where she wouldn't have to concentrate. Her mind could go to the warm space she had created with Rodney. It didn't matter that she knew nothing about him, whether he was a married man or even a paid gigolo.

When Kyle noted her feet were not in the right spot in the dinghy, and when she was too slow getting the anchor up, and later when she pinned the wet clothes on the safety lines in the wrong direction for optimal drying, she didn't even care. She had freed her spirit. "I'm trying," she said to Kyle. She adopted his ideal for her, without mocking. "I want to be the best sailor I can be."

That evening she climbed to the point of the V-berth and took Kyle's penis into her mouth.

"Move a little toward starboard," Kyle said. That meant

he wanted her to lie with her breasts on his right thigh.
She pushed herself against him without stopping the
movement of her head. She didn't think about what she
was doing. It was her usual routine in a boat in the middle
of nowhere with a husband who had all the answers and
all the questions. She felt his stiffness tighten and knew
he was coming. She automatically added her hand on his
"tiller" and slipped her mouth off in the last second before
she pumped him out. Then she held tight until he relaxed.
It was how he had trained her. She grabbed a handful of
Kleenex and swabbed his deck, as he liked to say.

"Umm. Thanks. Your turn tomorrow," Kyle said. In
seconds the snoring started.

Regina got up to throw away the tissues and lit one of
the kerosene lamps in the galley. Kyle wouldn't want her
draining the battery by turning on a light, even though the
wind generator and solar panels always provided plenty of
power. Conserve, conserve. Nothing is ever enough when
you can't get more.

She sat naked on a bunk in the soft glow and closed her
eyes against the burn of the kerosene fumes. She landed
herself right into Rodney's household. It was a small
concrete block place on the rocky beach of West End, with
no giant TV, no pool or Jacuzzi, no dock for a Pearson,
maybe a dog or even a child running around. Whose child?
She was sitting next to Rodney on a rattan sofa, feeling the
breeze through the screen door, watching a pink sunset out
the living room window.

It was ridiculous. What would she do in West End?
There certainly wasn't any work, even if Rodney was free
and interested in her. She wouldn't want to give up her
administrative assistant position at the community college.

Rodney was only a fantasy, but she enjoyed the feeling.

She opened the locker where Kyle kept his nail clippers and unzipped the leather pouch. Up on deck she hurled the clippers as far as she could and heard a plunk as they hit the water and sank to the sandy turtle grass bottom. They would corrode, no matter how sturdy the metal. For some reason it gave her pleasure.

The next day she woke up happy again. Kyle's complaints couldn't spoil her mood. Together they motored to shore in the dinghy and bought fresh conch from some Bahamians who had brought hundreds in their power boat to clean them at the deserted dock. Regina looked at the brown arms and long, dark dreadlocks on the man who handed her the conchs. Each time she reached for a slippery, rubbery handful of mollusk, she felt the warmth of his hand.

She took her Joy bath that day in the dinghy, whipping her hair into froth with a few drops of the yellow liquid, smearing a white sheen over her body. She was now an even brown from so much time of having no necessity for clothes, and sleek from burning calories just maintaining balance on the boat. She smoothed her slippery breasts and thought how beautiful she was.

Kyle didn't notice the missing clippers. That night she dumped a pair of his Sperry boat shoes with socks. He had two pairs anyway. The last night at Carter she filled a medium trash bag with his visor, Swiss Army knife, the last bottle of gin, his shaving lotion, favorite jockey shorts and a Tupperware container with hanks of lines, all neatly looped, that Kyle had been saving for years. The sound of the package hitting the water gave Regina a peace she never knew before. She didn't feel guilty. She was tidying

up—less to make a mess. A place for everything and
everything in its place. Kyle could do without all that stuff.

He had set the alarm for six, before first light, so they
could make it to their next destination, Green Turtle Cay.
There they would dock to fill up on fuel and water and
socialize with other sailing couples.

Kyle complained he couldn't find his shaving lotion.

"I don't know, honey," Regina said. "Maybe you set the
bottle on deck and it got knocked over."

"You know I always put everything back in its place."
He looked for his other pair of boat shoes that morning
also. Regina watched him search and wonder at himself.
He put on his damp shoes.

It was a cloudy, gusty day, winds reaching over twenty-
five knots, according to Kyle's calculations. He put three
reefs in the main and hooked up the storm jib that was
hardly bigger than a hanky. They were on a run like before,
only faster. It was an exhilarating ride. Regina watched the
clouds blow away in front of them as they flew. Kyle was
quiet for once, maybe enjoying himself. Suddenly the sun
came out full and hot on their backs and faces.

"Regina, get my visor from the locker above the chart
table."

She went down and started rummaging, knowing it
was gone. She noticed she was whistling.

"I can't find it, honey. Did you put it back last time?"

"Yes, I certainly did. I don't understand it." He paused
to think.

"Yes, dear."

"Regina, I'm going to give you the tiller for thirty
seconds while I look. You just aren't seeing it." He put his
finger under her chin to bring her head up. "Remember

what we learned the last time—about handling the tiller on a run?"

She nodded and smiled. "I know exactly what to do," she said.

Kyle stepped down the companionway and she swung the tiller hard to port, bracing herself. The boom slammed across with a crack like lightening. She thought the whole mast was going to topple, but it held.

Kyle's obscenity roared from below. She looked down and he was flopped across the settee. His eyes were glazed and his face was comic with anger. She wondered if he'd hit his head.

"You jibed!" he yelled. "You fucking jibed again!"

Regina smiled. A lunatic grin strained at her cheeks. She held the tiller alee, then brought it back amidships, and trimmed the sheets for a broad reach.

"What are you doing?" Kyle screamed. "Trying for a knock-down?"

"I was thinking I might, but I hate to get everything wet. Remember the time you did it?"

Kyle's eyes widened and he started to choke.

"Regina, get me those pills. Please. Dilantin—on the shelf by the binoculars. I can't get up."

Regina put her hands on her hips. "Please, you said? You've fallen and you can't get up?"

Regina trimmed the sails and tied the tiller so the *Spring Fling* would hove to. She reached the shelf inside the cabin without leaving the cockpit. "Here they are, sweetheart," she said. "What should I do now? See, Kyle, I'm asking—like you always tell me to do."

She heard a gurgle. He was lying flat on his back staring through the hatch at her.

She held up the pills. The bottle flipped from her hand and flew portside, almost by itself. She couldn't distinguish a splash with the wind and slapping waves, but the Dilantin was gone. "Oops," she said.

She listened to the noises coming from his throat. Kyle seemed to be listening and offering suggestions.

"I'd need to put on my snorkeling gear. I could also look for your nail clippers and favorite underwear—but I'm afraid they're long gone. Maybe you'd like to go in after them?"

Kyle started to shake violently, his arms and legs hyper-extending, drool running down his neck. Regina went up to release the jib and pull it down.

She returned and glanced into the cabin. Kyle's head was lolling on the back of the settee, eyes wide open. His body was slumped partly onto the sole.

She slipped down the companionway and felt the side of his neck for a pulse. There wasn't any, neither was there the sickening odor of his aftershave.

She turned on the VHF and picked up the microphone. Channel sixteen came on automatically. She pressed the button and yelled hysterically. "Mayday! Mayday! This is the *Spring Fling.* Need assistance immediately." She let up on the button and waited. No response. She tried again. "Mayday! Mayday!"

This time she got an answer. It was a sailboat west of Carter, from where she had come. She told them in a frantic voice that the captain was unconscious and she was an inexperienced mate. They responded that they would keep trying to reach the Bahamian Air Rescue. She told them she'd get her position from the GPS. She thanked them, her voice shaking.

Regina turned the boat into the wind, went forward and dropped the main, then returned to the cockpit and started the engine in neutral. She got out the GPS, which Kyle only allowed for emergencies, locked in the satellites, noted her position, and got the waypoint for Carter on the route to West End. She adjusted her compass course and pushed the throttle forward until she had 2,000 RPM's, as recommended. The engine was tuned perfectly as Kyle always kept it. This was surely emergency use.

She knew the Bahamian Rescue team would be there in no time to take Kyle's body. She was on her way back to Rodney, taking her chance, a big one, leaving her wealthy lifestyle behind. But without Kyle, Rodney didn't matter so much. She didn't need to think of his hand on her hair or his living room glowing in the sunset.

She went forward, rolled the sail and secured the ties with square knots. She knew it wouldn't be neat enough for Kyle. She glanced down at his body, staring wide-eyed from the settee, silent for once. She hooked the GPS to the auto-pilot—no need for more steering practice—and went below. She pulled out the sail cover and tied it down one last time, over Kyle's dead body.

Stepping back on deck she saw that the Dilantin bottle had caught at the port gunwale and was rolling along the deck.

She opened the bottle and took one pill to Kyle. "Here, I found them. They weren't in their place." She peeled the sail cover from his face, opened his teeth, and put a tablet on his bloody tongue. She closed his jaw. A tear dropped from her eye to Kyle's cheek, but she felt no regret.

She grabbed a beer from the fridge and went back to the cockpit and stretched out across a cushion. The engine was soothing with its loud rhythm. She relaxed, confident in her ability to make the two-day run to West End.

Sinny and the Prince

Once upon a time, nothing but pure pleasure here in twin-sis Lydia's palace on the Florida Intracoastal. Cindy in paradise, that's me—called myself Sinny in the trade. Sun slashing through palms, the slap of waves at the sea wall after a yacht passes by. A sweet, rotting smell of jungle, hanging orchids, giant-leaf plants and ferns, deep privacy. Orchid plants look dead, but according to Hudson, Lydia's new husband, Hudson Prince, the orchids are healthy and plenty rare. Don't touch!—as if I would.

Steel drum music on surround sound, water spurting over rock into the free-form pool. I'm itty-bitty-bikinied on my throne, Lydia's floating chair, smearing on coconut sun block, a salt-rimmed margarita in the drink holder—or a mojito—depending. Often a joint in my left hand, Lydia's creamy, high quality stuff. It's a land of milk and honey, far from the assholes who follow naturally pouty lips, big tits, and tight pussy on Bourbon Street. Ha! Goodbye to my old tricks, no more cunt-popping ping-pong balls into a net—hit the bull's-eye, ring a damn bell.

Me, the unlucky half of identical twins, got stuck with Mom and heroin, when Lydia fetched a high price from the rich lawyer, the household where Mom did the cleaning. A couple years later, when my little Cindy-ass

slowed Mom down on the biker scene, she dumped me
fast for nothing. Sure, I'd love it, a foster family with a real
dad, perfect, according to the state of Ohio.

Me, raped at ten. Lydia, ballet and piano in the music
room of her childhood mansion. Not her fault that at an
early age, I learned to take a finger up the wazoo without a
peep. It got me ice creams. And no, it didn't stop there. It
never does. So that's the tale, one princess and one pauper,
an old story. No excuse for murder, I know!

Desperate at twenty-six, when Katrina cleaned out
my life in one huge surge, I gambled my victim money on
a PI, and hit big-time when he found sis. In a heavy New
Orleans accent—to contrast with hers—told her and
Huddy-boy how I lost my Gulf Coast bed and breakfast,
barely escaped alive (one part true). So lucky to find my
sweet, generous sister when the whole world was swept
away.

As her twin, so easy to memorize Lydia's habits, get her
signature down pat. The change to Lydia's speech, my real
Midwest voice again after I kill her—piece of cake.

So here I am, the day before the deadly step, my eyes
closed, legs wide open astride the floating chair, feet
dangling in the warm water. I review, testing myself on
facts and Lydia's mannerisms, but mostly wallowing in
decadence.

The glass door slides open and shut. My guess, athletic
Hudson in his skimpy Speedo, ready for an after-work
swim, while Lydia downs a few drinks first at her leopard-
print decorated bar. Hud oozes sleaze, a world I know,
through $300 Hawaiian shirts he can afford with Lydia.
Slap of flip-flops, scratch of toenails on terrazzo, prancing
Lulu, the rat-sized dog. It's a better life for the spoiled

pooch than I ever had. I don't look, hope Hud goes away. Flip-flops cross the patio, pause . . . the whoosh of him . . . a wave . . . a splash!

"Fuck!" I wipe the water from my face, check the roach in the ashtray. Wet.

He laughs. "Thought you were dead, Cindy, finally overdid the booze and sun."

Remember the accent. "Ya'll would spla-ash a corpse, Hud?"

"Not as a rule, but you, yes." He shakes the water from his curly, shoulder length hair, diamond ear stud catching light. "Hudson. Not Hud."

I shut my eyes, reject the bait from Prince Sorry-Piece-of-Shit married to the money. Lydia must be dreaming if she thinks he's in love. He's using, leaching funds for a business that neither will talk about. Some scam he knows I'll see through, so he's sworn her to secrecy. She's wrapped around his finger, but she's not stupid. With her kind of money, and lawyers, there's a pre-nup for sure. When I'm Lydia, I'll divorce Hud's ass, collect the house and bank account—which must be huge since the old adopted mother passed. Palm Beach society folk, according to the obit. Sweet Lydia. She wouldn't say *shit* if she had a mouthful. At least, that's her act. An easy act in a life of fantasy.

"How much longer you plan to stay?" Hud asks. He's back-stroking with his head above water.

"Soon as I fah-nd a job, get paid, I'm out a he-ah."

"Fish and guests, you know—three days tops. You've been here three weeks already." He laughs and pauses mid-stroke to pinch his nose for emphasis. "Time to start hustling that pussy."

I don't know if he suspects my real career or is just being crude. I ignore him, since he doesn't matter. Everything is Lydia's.

He reaches the side, ducks, flips over, and swims the length of the pool under water. If only I could kill *him* instead.

That evening at dinner Lydia is the princess, for sure. Hair swept up, gold and pearls dripping from her ears, a pale blue kimono—pure silk, I bet. Make-up perfect, full glossy lips, long lashes brushing soft, powdered cheeks. She smiles, pours the wine, her dimple showing. She's exactly like me, yet so lovely that I want to kiss her. But I don't know her and I never will. The longer the wait, the harder murder gets. She passes *foie gras* on a chilled sterling platter. No goose safe from the moneyed.

I hand the dish to Hudson. Only meatless meals for Sinny, to set up more differences between me and Lydia. I'm anemic waiting to make the switch! Even Lulu has a tender bite of liver in her crystal dog dish under the table.

"We have to go out tonight, Cindy. A charity event. Too late to get a ticket for you."

She's too embarrassed for me to meet her friends. "Shu-ah, Lydie, but we nev-ah get to talk."

Hudson turns my way, on the side Lydia can't see, a silent snarl.

Lydia chews a tiny bite, gulps her wine. "I know."

I nod, eager to have the place to myself at night, watch the giant-screen TV with five-hundred channels, sipping Grand Marnier and nibbling left-over liver before it becomes Lulu food. More luxury in one evening than for my whole life till now.

"Tomorrow Hudson can handle business alone. We'll

spend the afternoon together—girl talk."

My stomach drops. I lift the wine glass to hide my feelings. This is the chance I've been waiting for.

Chef Phillip serves them filet mignon with black peppercorns, and me a cheesy vegetable soufflé. I try to finish my mushroom bisque, act normal.

"We'll all go out to eat at The Forge," Lydia says. "Take the afternoon off tomorrow, Phillip."

I smile. "Fa-an-ta-stic." But I know we'll never make it. Time alone with Lydia is time to kill her. As always, I check her napkin—reinforcing—the way it's folded, her dabbing at her lips. She eats clockwise round her plate, switching knife and fork, cutting filet. I eat left-handed— until tomorrow night. Thinking of the plan, I can hardly swallow.

The maid removes the plates, and Lydia serves herself more wine. She's had three glasses, from appetizer to dessert, scotch straight up before dinner. I can't imagine what part of this fairy tale she's drinking to forget, but her problem makes my luck.

At noon the next day, Phillip serves us lunch on the patio, a salad with pears and blue cheese, sugared pecans tossed on top. We toast with champagne. It helps me get the food down. Phillip and the maid leave soon after. I want to forget the plan and go to the restaurant for dinner, but I'll lose my nerve if I wait longer. Cindy's days are numbered in this household, one way or another.

"To twins, happy together," Lydia toasts.

"I owe you so much, Sis-ta."

She shakes her head and drinks up, lips scrunched to her nose, meaning it's nothing—an expression I've practiced in the mirror, too cute for words.

I can do this. There's no choice. I'll make up for it, become an even better Lydia, innocent and giving to the core—after the divorce. The world won't miss Cindy, and Lydia will live on.

After lunch, I bring out a box of dye, the auburn color I have on my hair. Our hair is equal length, but mine's curled tight to seem shorter. Only the finest salons have touched Lydia's do, but she agrees to let me dye it, for sisterly bonding.

"It'll be fun to look a-lahk," I say, "and it's a tenth the pr-ahce of a salon."

"You get what you pay for," she tells me, wagging her finger.

"Not always, Shuga. Sometimes you get mo-ah." I point to my own auburn head. "Ah know what ah'm doin with this."

Upstairs, she smokes some weed, while I section her hair and squeeze on the gel. We talk about her life, her past, the loving adopted family, some aunts and uncles. Even high, she won't say a word about Hud's business. We finish the champagne, waiting for the color to work. She washes her hair, and I blow it dry in her normal way, parted in the middle and curved toward her face, a style I'll soon enjoy. She kisses me on the cheek and says thanks, but I can tell she's not thrilled.

I take her hand. "How 'bout some drinks by the pool? Ah fix a great mah-ga-rita."

We sit at the umbrella table by the waterfall and talk. She drinks, I sip. I tell her about my childhood, and tears well in her eyes. I can almost believe she's real. Her act would break my heart if it wasn't smashed to pieces long ago. I drink up, soak in more details—still nothing about the business. She starts to slur.

"Let's take a dip," I tell her.

We change into our bikinis and I make her another strong margarita. We sit in the pool on the concrete steps. She talks, I don't listen. Finishes her drink fast. Blotto.

Now or never. I take her by the arm. She smiles, her glassy eyes helping to convince me that it won't hurt. She'll never know what happened, as they say.

Pull her into the shallow water, sweep her feet with one leg, whack her head hard on the second step. The crack of bone on concrete jars me, brings up bile in my throat. I pull her up by the hair, turn her over to look at her face. She's limp, her eyes closed, mouth slack. A trickle of blood down the side of her nose drips into the pool. She's out, no struggle, no going back. Lift one eyelid, look into the eye's vacant stare. Don't know if she's dead, but the worst is over. Lulu comes running, high-pitched yapping, yapping. Splash her and she runs away.

Push Lydia down with the flat of my hand on her chest, hold her there. A hazy blood-cloud sweeps between my thighs, and bubbles follow, the flow from her mouth. I bite my lip, call up cruelties from childhood to blunt my feelings, ease my stomach, emotions I wasn't expecting. I didn't create evil in the world, just one action in a lifetime of it. Bubbles stop. Take no chances. I hold her ten minutes under water, by the clock, trying to calm my pulse and breath, think of the clothes, luxuries, the crown of respect I'll have living in her skin.

I pull her head up gently, look at her vacant face, the pink gash and loose white edges of skin, imagine it's me, Cindy. For all purposes, it soon will be.

I unhook the bra of her bikini, strip it off lovely breasts,

perfect pink nipples. Trail my fingers across them slowly—
just like mine, but satin. I hold her to my body, her head
on my shoulder, feel her coolness, slip my hand down the
front of her bottoms, find the last of her warmth inside.
"I'm sorry, Lydia. I'm sorry, so sorry." I might have made
a huge mistake. She's headed for a better place, but think
how close we might have been!

I lean her on the steps, head lolling. Finish, before
Hudson gets home. Take a deep breath. Grab her legs. It's
awkward. She slips down. Balance her across my thigh to
keep her head from hitting concrete again. Take off her
bottoms, one leg at a time. Her pubic hair is shaved into a
Mohawk. I turn her over, look at the same ass I've seen in
mirrors. Every part exact, heredity perfect. No birthmarks
or moles I'd have to fake for Hudson. A few light freckles
on her lower back. Florida sun. No way he'll notice.

I let her down lightly onto the bottom, strip off my suit,
and put on hers. Pull the body back across my knee, hook
my bra around her waist, twist, drop arms through loops,
lift, and tuck. Slide up bottoms, gently, gently. Only my
hair to dye and pussy to shave.

I clean up the dye kit from her bathroom and take the
empty auburn box and bottles to throw away in mine. I dye
my hair black and tear the dye box into tiny pieces to flush,
rinse the bottle and toss it in the back of the cabinet until
later. No one should suspect anything, but I don't take
chances. I let my hair dry straight, dress in one of her silky
gowns and crawl into the sheets. The pillow is heavy with
the smell of her. I roll to the other side of the bed, holding
back tears so my eyes won't be red, pretending to nap until
Hudson finds "Cindy" dead in the pool.

The ambulance comes, the police. No problem for

me to sob real tears. I suck it up and answer questions. An accident. There's no motive, no reason to investigate. Cindy dove in, drunk, hit her head and drowned while I was asleep. No known friends, other relatives, or acquaintances. It's all so easy. The pauper's death is even less important than she thought.

More tears that night. Let them flow. Hudson is quiet, but I know he's celebrating in his head. The nasty Cindy gone. He stays downstairs, doing paperwork or drinking. I go up, glad to leave his sight. Slip into the silk nightgown from behind the bathroom door and spend some time looking at Lydia's jewelry, earrings and bracelets, daily wear in the box on the dresser, but I'm sure there's more in a safety deposit box. Her drawers are filled with lingerie, silk and lace, fancy garter belts, leather thongs and cut out bras, a major shopping habit. Her nightstand with more. On Hudson's side a cock ring and lubes. Ugh. I know I have him to look forward to. Farther back a Glock, like the one I lost to Katrina with everything else. Rounds in the clip. No surprise from the prince.

I go to the antique desk, where she keeps her mail, the drawer filled with letters from charities, cancelled checks for donations of thousands, and requests for more. I slide open the roll-top. Full of photos. Little girls, several, from third world countries, smiling, showing new dresses, storybooks. My eyes well up.

I hear Hudson on the stairs and close the drawer. Want him to think I'm sleeping, but once I'm in bed, Lydia's scent brings out full sobs. Hudson comes in, slides under the sheets naked. Lulu hops up, sniffs me, wanders down to his feet.

"Cindy's in a better place," he says and pats my head.

He turns away, curls up, and snores. Good thing, or I would've puked.

The next few days I play my part. Easy to be the grieving Lydia, since I'm sad and guilty. I help him put together a small funeral, get through it. The morning after, Hud wakes me with his hand between my legs. I look at him. Soft-skinned, square-jawed, thick hair. Tan and attractive, charming, but I hate him. I pull off the sheet and scoot toward the edge.

He grabs my gown, pulls me back on the pillow. "A quickie," he says.

No escape. I have to make this work a while, move gradual toward divorce. His mouth turns toward me, warm lips cover mine, a forceful tongue. Not caring much for men, I've had years of practice faking. His fingers find my slit and stroke it none too gently. I don't react, since Lydia is still upset, but he climbs on top and pushes in.

Speed suits me. He grins and pumps, groans, rolls off onto his back. He laughs, a throaty quiet sound, catches his breath, laughs some more. I want to ask what's so hysterical, but it might be a habit that Lydia can't question. I've seen men chuckle when they come, just not this much.

"It feels so good," he says. "We have to do this more."

"I'm not myself," I tell him. "Give me some time."

"You're fine." He rolls close to face me, tweaks my dimple. "I need you at the studio today."

"The studio? Already?"

"You'll feel much better—take your mind off . . . Cindy."

"Not yet."

"Okay, tomorrow then."

He taps my head. "I'll need the check for eighty thou.

The rest next week."

"Oh?" I say.

"The new camera, more lights."

I know he's scamming, but I can't catch him. Can't go
back on Lydia's word. Lydia. Sweet Lydia. "No problem."

He brings the checkbook from the desk. I write it out
like the cancelled checks I've memorized.

The next day I dress in a casual outfit I saw on Lydia
when she left with him one morning. I'm nervous on the
drive, despite Hud's Mercedes convertible —another of
his toys, like the Harley, the Wave-Runner, and a growing
gun collection, all compliments of Lydia. He's mentioned
shopping for a yacht. Not on my money, greedy piece of
shit!

We turn into a warehouse district, pull up to a concrete
building with no sign. A few cars are parked on the side. If I
can't do the work, I'll fake illness till I learn.

The door is unlocked. An office. Hudson follows. A
desk and computer, some metal files. Two girls in low cut
jeans, with naval rings and skimpy tops, together on a black
leather couch, talk close enough to feel each other's breath.
Dancers—strippers—I know the type.

Follow Hudson through the door. Lights, two cameras,
all aimed toward a king-sized bed. Impossible. I just
escaped this world. Not Lydia!

"Get ready," he tells me and gestures down the hall.

I nod, walk past some doors, open the one stenciled
"Lydia" in black paint. Inside, lighted make-up mirror, an
open closet filled with lingerie, short skirts, thin shirts,
fishnet stockings, and pairs of spike heels. On the back
of the chair, a costume—a short, high-bodiced, blue
transparent gown, a crown, and on the floor, clear plastic

stilettos. Looks like "Sinny as Cinderella." My old act, back to haunt me. But Lydia? In this? How's that for nature over nurture?

I take off my clothes, slip on a garter belt, stockings, white lace bra, the gown, heels, stare at the crown. No choice. Play along. I've done this for much less.

The lights are blazing when I come back out. Naked hunk on the edge of the bed is worked up big-time, watching the girls from the office cuddle, my stepsisters in skimpy tatters, moist skin gleaming in the lights. Them I don't mind. Don't see a fairy godmother with her magic wand.

I set the crown on a stool.

"Put it on," Hud says and points. "In the middle, down on all fours."

"Oh, yes," I say. "Forgot where we were." I clip on the crown, crawl across the bed, heading for the girls. The hot lights warm my skin, all so familiar.

Camera guys adjust their lights. Hud steps forward. "Action!"

Spread legs before me, the smell of cunt perfume. I take my pick of pussy and tuck my face in happily, but soon the hunk pulls me back for the hetero shot, flips the gown over my back, and plugs me. Set thoughts on foie gras and champagne, body on automatic.

"Cut!"

The cock stops. Hud leans close, grinning, all teeth, in the spot lights. He motions toward my ass. "Let's have an anal shot, Big Dan. When we start again, move up."

"You got it."

"Get me some lube," I say.

"No lube. We're out."

Dan spits into his palm, spreads on the saliva.

"Make it pretty," Hud says and winks. "Action!"

I clench my teeth against the burn, turn pain into
passion on face level. Nothing new for me. But why would
Lydia ? . . .

That night we dine on lobster and risotto, fresh
asparagus crusted with Parmigiano Reggiano, bread
pudding with bourbon sauce for dessert. I tell myself it's all
worthwhile and won't last long, but between buttery bites
of lobster and mouthfuls of dry white wine, I'm angry and
depressed. Hud's chatter makes me sick.

I eat around my plate, dab my napkin, every gesture
reminding me that I'm an act, not a person, a mirror image,
no guts. I gulp my wine, thank God for her drinking.

I get up from the table, brush his cheek with a kiss,
walk toward the stairs, swallow what's stuck in the back of
my throat. "I'm tired and sore."

"I have to make some calls. Be up in a while," he says.

A warm soak, gardenia scented oil, a bath pillow and
low jazz. Candles flickering on polished marble, and thick,
Egyptian cotton towels waiting on the heated rack. It's
mine. All mine. The worst is over. Lydia will soon give Hud
the boot, retire from porn.

I get into bed, catch the scent of the princess from her
feather pillow, think about the pea that could be tucked
under the mattress. I've felt worse under me – on me
– in me, but I'm jittery from being a fake. Life might have
been wonderful without the plan, loving Lydia, instead of
memorizing her details.

Hud comes in late, all booze and cigar, reaches under
the sheet and smacks my ass. I try to roll away, but he grabs
me around the waist, pulls up my gown and clamps me to

the bed, my arms and shoulders under his thighs.

"Hud, stop!"

"You love it, wench! Let's see you struggle."

Lydia, S and M? I twist myself and claw at the bed, but his full weight is on me. I'm smothering, and I don't know their word for stop. Gown comes off, a long scarf goes across my open mouth, is knotted behind my head.

He reins me back with a jerk, slaps my ass hard, again and again. "You love it, you love it, you love it." A whack for each time he says love.

I growl in my throat while he grunts and whoops.

I'm gasping for breath when he lifts my hips, shoves inside where I'm already sore, whacking and pumping. I clench my fists and groan. Why, Lydia?

Finally, he comes, drops down on top of me, laughs until he rolls aside and snores.

The next morning we stop at the bank. He comes back with a manila envelope, stuffed. On the way to the studio he tells me he's got a special set up for the day. "Triple our money," he says. "You help. No need to get undressed."

We pull up to the building, near a taxi. A woman gets out. Sickly thin, limp hair, dark circles under the eyes, a crack whore who's been at it for years. She lights up a cigarette and reaches into the cab, yanks out a girl, maybe ten years old, in a short pink dress.

I lose my balance walking past, bounce against the Mercedes.

Hud looks at me. I turn my back and go inside. No! Lydia would never! I must be wrong.

In the dressing room I look around. Open cabinets. Yeah, there's a bottle, vodka, half full. I gulp until it numbs my brain, take air, and gulp some more. This can't be happening.

I walk into the studio. See Hud from behind, his toned ass in tiny black briefs on the bed. I'm running now. The pink dress is on the floor. I stop outside the cameras, stare into the blinding light. She's all ribs and boney knees, eyes dilated, a drugged child with a red-hooded cape down her back and smiley-face underpants. Hud strokes her small thigh with one finger.

"Stop it!" I scream. I leap onto the bed, grab his hand, push at his bare chest, yank his arm. "No! Not this."

"Cut!" he says and turns to me with his sneer. He's wearing a snout. Pulls it off. "What's the matter with you?"

He grabs a black robe from the chair, pushes me ahead of him into the outer hall.

"Lydia would never allow this!" I yell.

"Lydia wouldn't?"

"I won't," I say. "I won't allow this. I'll call the police!"

He whispers into my ear. "You're right. Lydia wouldn't, but you will, Cindy."

My stomach is a rock.

He laughs that irritating laugh, deeper, more penetrating. I make a fist, a shot to his gut, but he grabs my wrist, and I don't even touch him. Hits me in the mouth with his other hand. Blood runs. I suck it up, swallow it down.

He pins me to the wall. "It was a hard decision, whether to turn you in or play you." He smirks. "But I've been enjoying this."

"What the hell are you talking about, Hudson?"

"Been doing your Kegel exercises, huh, sweetums? Toning the merchandise? I knew it was you the first time we fucked. You're one sweet cunt, Cindy."

"You're insane," I say, but there's no happy ever after in my future. The evil sister's slipper fits too tight. Betrayed by the muscle I'd worked so hard, when bull's eyes made the money.

He laughs, shakes his head. "You thought you'd fool me and get away with this shit?"

"I'll divorce you, Hud. You won't get a cent."

"Oh, yeah? Heard of dental records, smart ass? Lydia's teeth are perfect."

The detail I forgot. He shoves me against the wall and pries open my jaw to the dark silver on top. Doesn't matter. I already opened my mouth too wide.

He breathes in my face, laughs. "Lydia never performed. She kept a hand in the books—and her eye on me." He pokes my dimple. "Now I'm in control."

"No!"

He clamps his hand across my mouth. "Do what I say or I call homicide."

I seethe. His grin widens, white teeth bared. "It's a great deal for you, Cindy, if you behave. Go home, relax. All I need is money."

He drops his hand and lets me go. I run to the dressing room, grab my purse, call a taxi. I pass through the studio, its dark edges. Crack Momma and the little girl, she's dressed, eating a popsicle. They walk toward the door, Hud talking to the mother, paying from his wad of cash. Back at the bed, a "step-sister" dons the red cape. I helped this child today, but it won't end. When Ma's high runs out, she'll remember his money.

I can't call the cops. They come sniffing around, I'm fried. Hud inherits all. No way, bastard Prince!

I get home, send off Phillip and the maid, feed Lulu

to get her out from underfoot. Pull on a bikini, grab the
Glock, head down to the patio bar. Take the full bottle of
Glenlivet to my spot on the edge of the pool, position the
gun under a towel, pointed toward the steps. No more
elaborate plans—soak my feet and drink, shoot him, shoot
me.

I wait, I sip, go for the numbness. The hours pass, a
long time to dwell on stupidity and keep enough mind to
squeeze the trigger twice.

Dusk, a half-bottle down. The glass door slides open,
then shut. Flip-flops and the scratch of Lulu coming close.

"So, Cindy," he says, "Here we are." He stops, slips
off his shoes, walks to the steps and down, closer, closer.
"I see you've helped yourself to my best scotch. I'll allow
that—today."

I grab the gun, two-handed, aim straight, and squeeze.
Gut-shot, he spouts blood in the water. Another blast to
throat, then chest. He slides down too quick for the long
look I would've enjoyed. A blood cloud drifts across my
feet. Lulu is yapping in my ear. Aim the gun at her bug-
eyed head. No!

I lean toward my reflection on the water, tuck the
straight dark hair behind my ear, and contemplate my
second death, this time a suicide.

Take the barrel to my lips. Suck in a last breath. "Fuck!"
I cough. Gunpowder residue, the sting of cinders, what
else? I cough and cough, set the gun down. Smack Lulu's
butt to make her run. Swig Glenlivet. Pick up the gun and
touch metal to my ear. I'm coming, Lydia. To make it all
up . . . .

Finger won't move. Set down the gun, lift the bottle. A
long gulp. I rub my eyes, sniff, wipe the snot from my nose,

look at the gun on the terrazzo. Touch my lip. It's swollen from the punch. I work the bruised jaw, look at bastard Prince down at the bottom, under a dark haze of lingering blood. Child pornography and abuse. Self-defense? Lydia can afford the best lawyers.

I slug the Glenlivet, feel the burn. Suicide is not in our genes.

Sweet Dreams

Henry must've thought old bats like Granny and me hadn't been poked in a decade or two so we'd gladly hike our nighties for a moment of bliss, and then he could eat our food and smoke our dope for the rest of his life. He was pretty much right, I guess, but it didn't work out how any of us had planned.

He turned up one spring evening with a bottle of Chardonnay when we were a tad high, relaxing on our front porch. That was our regular evening activity. I was a widow for years, and Granny had never married. She was nobody's grandma, but I nicknamed her after the old gal from "Beverly Hillbillies." Gran was an Olympic swimmer and women's swim team coach, mostly in the years before good sunscreen was invented. I had that leathery sheen myself, being the first female lifeguard for the City of Ft. Lauderdale. We were both Florida crackers, and when we met at the Hall of Fame Pool nearly twenty years ago we became instant friends and soon housemates.

Nowadays our lives weren't too exciting, both of us being seventy-somethings. Our pensions were small, but we'd bought a half acre of property out in Davie, Florida, before the prices went up, so we had some space, and fed eight to ten sweet kitties, depending on which day you

were counting. We could afford basic cable, and once a
month or so, we risked a drive over to the beach to swim.
Also belonged to a ladies' poker club. We grew patches of
tomatoes, zucchini, and Maryjane in the back—for our
own use. We made sure to smoke a little dope at least once
a day, to fight off the glaucoma. It sure worked. Neither
of us had any signs of the disease. Gran had only taken to
smoking with me in her old age, but pot linked back to
my wild youth and the Beats. Every time I rolled one, I
thought of my poet husband with his beret and earrings,
and how happy we felt, just hanging out together, no
money. We lived for dreams of the future that never came
true, but enjoyed ourselves along the way.

Now that the future was all downhill for Gran and
me, the weed helped relieve the boredom, made us forget
that the only unknown in our lives was which parts would
go bad first, our bodies or our brains. Of course, we were
thankful that we didn't have any debilitating diseases
as yet, but there was so much the two of us still wanted
to do. Like a trip to Hawaii. After a few tokes, it almost
seemed possible, zipping along the waves in a Zodiac from
Hanalei on the north coast of Kauai to scuba dive, where
dolphins frolicked in the wake and the water was clear as
air. It was all on *Discovery*, or maybe *Jacques Cousteau*, the
reefs with lionfish and clowns and huge Pacific corals and
sponges. I pictured myself weaving gracefully through a
dramatic forest of giant kelp, in total silence except for my
own bubbles—and Gran's. Diving was the one sport we
were still able to enjoy, but only locally, about once a year
because of the cost.

Some people settle in easy to old age, I guess,
enjoying their restaurant Early Bird Specials and Boca

cocktails—meaning free lemonade, made with a large water, extra lemons, and a packet of Sweet 'N Low. Me and Gran needed more than our pocketbooks would allow. Dreaming was damn futile, except when we were high. But then life served us up Henry, like a kick-start, and we got greedy.

That evening, when he dawdled across the road, I thought the smoke drew him over, or maybe the smell of pork roast and taters in the oven, but later I realized he must have been saving up his panhandlings for days, to buy that ten-dollar bottle. We recognized him from the bench at the bus stop, where he often slept one off. Couldn't blame him. For an old homeless man, living on hand-outs and dumpster fare, rot-gut was the only entertainment.

He seemed to believe he was a looker, but I doubt he was ever much above average. Then, add years on the street, cigarettes and alcohol. Eventually, he claimed to be a young buck of sixty-nine, but he looked older than us, bent over and rail thin, with shaky, cracked fingers and a wheeze. The rattiness of his clothes and scraggly beard made his homelessness obvious, but boy, he poured on the manners. He was wearing a baseball cap, and he tipped it. "Ladies," he said. He reminded me of a real beat up Jack Nicholson.

Granny looked at me, and we resigned ourselves to getting a pitch of some kind, leading to a handout. He walked right up on the porch, despite our glares.

"I was just noticing how lovely you girls look in your summer dresses."

Gran glanced toward me with her eyebrows up and mouth gaping. We were both wearing faded, cat-pulled chenille robes over our nighties. Gran had a mangy old calico snoring on her lap.

"Can I offer you ladies a glass of wine? I just bought this nice Chardonnay, and it's going to get warm before I can drink it all by myself." He was pointing toward the paper bag he held. The Seven-Eleven was a few blocks down, so it was probably true about the wine warming up, as if that would matter to him.

"I don't see no glasses," Granny said. "You just expect ladies to swig outta the bottle?" She turned to me. "What do you think of that, Lu?"

My throat was feeling scratchy and parched, and a soothing drink sounded like just the ticket. Gran had the cat, so I got up. "I'll get the juice glasses," I said and headed inside.

When I came out, ole Henry was on the swing next to where I'd been sitting, petting that calico real close to Gran's cooter. I set the glasses on the window sill so he'd have to get up to do the honors. When he did, I sat back down in the middle of the swing, so there wasn't enough room for him on either side. He could stand if he was so damn polite. He did.

He poured and we drank. At some point the pork roast got eaten.

Next morning, I woke up with a head ready to explode. I reached toward the night stand with my eyes closed to feel for my glass of water and I put a finger right into Henry's nostril. "Son of a bitch," I hollered.

He grabbed his nose and pulled at it, yowling—like I could've knocked it out of joint with that little tweak. He was grinning though, and even without my glasses, I could barely stand looking at his teeth, the few of them. That grin brought the whole night, or at least the disgusting parts, tumbling back into my brain.

"Get the hell outta my bed!"

"I'm fixed, Sweetie, so you don't have to worry about getting pregnant." He laughed and laughed.

"Get out!" I hollered.

He kept laughing and didn't budge. I stuck my hand under the covers and pushed. Ick. Cooties, I was thinking. He was naked, and his wrinkled ass felt like a greasy paper bag. I pushed and grunted, but finally he just raised up slow, all his bones creaking and cracking. He loomed close like he was going to kiss me, and I yanked the quilt up to cover my face. Thank god, I wasn't wearing my glasses because that scraggly face and bony chest were scary enough without having to focus on the dangling organ lower down, especially knowing where it had been—or maybe just tried to be.

"You sure as hell better not have AIDS," I hissed through the quilt.

He laughed so hard he started to cough. "How long you expecting to live anyway?" He laughed some more.

"Longer than you!" I stayed under the quilt listening to him get dressed until I heard his steps dragging down the hall toward the kitchen. I could've killed him, or myself. I was already itchy.

I smelled bacon, but decided to go back to sleep. My hope was that he'd leave when the bacon was gone.

I got up at noon, feeling pretty rocky. Walking past the window, I saw him out back watering the weed patch. Humph. Granny was in the living room locked into her stories on the big TV, but I stepped right in front of the screen and let her have it.

"Granny, what the hell you thinking of, letting that old

fart know about our crop? Now he's got something on us!"

She jerked left and right and waved me away, and I looked at the screen and saw one of those soap opera love scenes going on, fingers running through hair and mouths glued together. I didn't want to ruin her stories. I dropped into the La-Z-Boy and tried not to blow up until the commercial came on.

"Now what'd you say, Lulu?"

I repeated myself, but without much conviction. I could never stay mad at Granny for more than a minute.

"Don't get your panties aflutter, Lu. He just wants to help out in exchange for meals. We got lots around here that needs fixing. I'm making a list. You probably have some stuff needs doing too." She snickered.

I ignored it. "Not worth it. Definitely not worth it," I said. "He's gonna spoil what little we got going."

"I already told him he could sleep in the shed—unless you want to share your bed?" She cackled, and my hope that she was only guessing went down the drain. My neck got hot.

Her stories came back on, and I went into the kitchen to watch Henry through the window. Granny and me were halfsies on the house with survivorship rights, so I had as much say as she did, but I never went up against her. Maybe Henry would get sick of us shortly and head off of his own free will.

My wish was not granted. Two months went by, and he still hung around. He didn't bother me in bed any more, but he was sleeping in the shed on an air mattress a few nights a week, taking showers in our bathroom, using hair products, and managing to get a meal or two out of us daily. I could tell he was into the peanut butter and jelly

when we weren't looking. He played it cool in front of
Granny, but to me there were innuendoes that if I didn't
act nice to him, he'd rat about the "illegal substance." He
was always on my nerves and costing us extra food money,
and he left pubic hairs on the soap.

Meanwhile, there was another problem. Granny
had forgot to fill out her Medicare forms and her blood
pressure drugs were draining our entertainment fund, so
by the third month, we were either gonna have to cut the
cable or the meat budget—or Henry. That wasn't going
to be easy. I was feeling desperate. One morning I read
in the paper about some old ladies who scammed their
insurance company by taking out life insurance on a bum.
They forged his signature, and then killed him, just ran him
over with a stolen car. Brilliant. Now, after being connected
with three homeless men that had been run over, the
women were being charged with murder. But Granny and
me only needed to pull it off once. The problem was, since
it had already been done, the insurance companies were
bound to be checking up on the beneficiaries. Hell—I
could marry the bum and make the new policy legit. He
wouldn't have any objections, considering that would
guarantee his meals. It would be a short marriage.

I was still thinking about it a few nights later when
Granny and me were sitting on the couch and the old fart
was on the La-Z-Boy. It was Gran's turn in the chair, but
somehow he beat her to it, and she didn't say anything.
Usually, he was passed out by then. We were watching
Discovery, a pile of crocodiles eating zebras when they tried
to cross the river, a bloody thrashing for prime time. I don't
know if the violence turned Henry on, or if he was just too
far gone to realize, but he was playing with himself, right

there in our living room. I watched him out of the corner
of my eye for a few minutes, finding it humorous the way
his shaky fingers curled around his penis and jerked up
and down. He had it working, but he needed Oil of Olay
or some such. His wiener still looked young when it was
full and stretched out. He was lucky with that, the gift that
keeps on giving.

Finally, Granny saw him. "What the hell! You got your
pud out in the living room?" she hollered.

I laughed out loud at her using that word.

Henry slapped his hands over his erection and started
to cough his lungs out, probably close to a heart attack.
Granny weighed ninety pounds, but she'd never lost her
volume from swim coach days.

"Ain't you learned to do that in private?" she bellowed.

He tucked it in and scuffled out the door to the shed, I
guess, to finish up.

"I know what to do about him," I said. I'd clipped some
articles from the *Sun Sentinel* and went to get them from
my room. I grabbed some rolling papers and a baggie of
private stock along the way. Gran read while I rolled. We
knew Henry had no living relatives because he whined
about it all the time. He'd been on the street or in flop
houses for years and hadn't even set up an address so he
could collect his Social Security. That's how smart he was.

"You serious? Kind of severe punishment for
masturbation," Gran said. "Who'd kill him?"

"I'll run him over. He's always drunk, so it'll be easy. I
figure I should marry him, to keep down suspicion. Also,
we'll have to steal a car."

"You'd marry him? That old penis-head?"

"I'd rather not, but it's better than getting caught. The

insurance companies are bound to be on the lookout."

"How much did those gals git?"

"Plenty." I handed her a second article and pointed. "On one old geezer alone, they got almost $400,000."

"Damn. Well, hell, I'll marry him then. You don't need to put yourself out. We only have to kill Henry and we'll be set up, even if we live to be a hunnerd."

"Huh, you want to marry him?"

"Well, I don't especially want to," she said, "but it won't be for long. You've been married, and I never have."

I shrugged. "Okay, then. How you gonna ask him?"

"No problem. I'll pretend I'm worried what the neighbors are saying."

"Guess he'll go for almost anything to get fed."

"What are you saying, Lu? That he don't find me attractive?"

I didn't know if she was serious or making a joke. I ignored her and looked back at the article. "It says the women kept the guys alive for two years, so the insurance companies wouldn't get suspicious. Maybe we can cut the time a little."

"Let's get on the ball—while we have enough spunk left to dive Hawaii."

I stuck out my hand and we high-fived. "Tiny bubbles," I sang and swished my hips back and forth, playing an air-ukulele, "in your eyes—or something like that. Meanwhile, we can get him to apply for Social Security and that'll cover his share of the household."

"I don't see any downside to this." Gran pulled a hair out of the mole on her chin. "Never thought I'd be marrying this late, but heck."

At the time, I thought I would be fine with Granny

taking the vows, but that night I woke up feeling lousy and realized that I wanted to be the wife. After all, Henry and me were the ones that had an encounter.

I could see Gran's light was on down the hall, and I decided to get the deal straightened out, instead of letting it eat at me.

I knocked on her door and opened it. "Jesus Christ!" I hollered. There in full light from the overhead was Gran completely naked, looking like a fryer too long in the fridge, and Henry in boxers with his grizzled face nudged up between her drumsticks.

"We're engaged!" she hollered.

Henry squatted his boney ass and raised his head, staring at me with drool on his chin.

It put me into a snit. It didn't seem no first-time coincidence. No wonder he felt so comfortable stroking his pecker in our living room. We'd both seen it before, just not together. Maybe that's what he wanted, both of us at once, egotistical old buzzard. And all this time, I'd assumed Gran was a lesbian. She'd had the right hair and shoes ever since I'd known her.

She whipped up the blanket over the two of them, thank god, Henry completely under the covers. "Jest fooling around. Henry wanted to show me something. I'll tell you all about it later."

I swallowed my bile, squinted, and made a mouth to indicate disgust, as I left the room. I decided I was too old and too smart to be jealous of my best friend over some drunken idiot we were just gonna kill.

In the morning when I got up he was back in the shed, and she was at the table having her toast with raspberry pepper jelly and coffee. She was chipper.

"Sit down, Lu, and have some breakfast. This is going to work out."

She told me they'd set the date for a week from Saturday, and she wanted me to send out invitations and be her matron of honor in my pale green chiffon with the sequins. I had it from my niece's wedding in '95. While I was still asleep, she'd already invited a couple women from our poker club for the ceremony and a potluck on Sat evening. "We'd better rent a canopy for the back yard in case of rain," she told me.

I was shocked that she wanted to make such a big to-do, but it sounded like fun and would throw off any suspicion.

"Would you make the cake, Lu? Please? It would mean a lot to me."

"Huh?" I said. I didn't expect her feelings to enter in. "We just want the insurance money, remember?"

"Shit, I know! But we need it to look real. It's not everyday an old bat like me gets married. The neighbors would wonder if we didn't do it up a little."

"I guess." We only had two neighbors within a quarter mile.

"You know I'd do anything for one of your fudge ribbon cakes, honey."

She started humming "Tiny Bubbles" and smiled at me, and I had no choice but to be a good sport. After all, I wanted Gran to be happy as much as I wanted to be happy myself. I could go along with the celebration. I didn't remember the last time I baked that cake, but I found the recipe and got busy making arrangements.

The wedding was a small affair, but nice. Gran had bought a sky blue suit with a frilly white blouse and

blue low heels to match, and I was in my green. Henry
had a shave and haircut and wore a suit Gran got him at
the Good Will. We did the ceremony at city hall in the
morning. Then the half-dozen old gals from the card club,
a few old farts that knew Henry from the bar down the
street, and the two neighbor couples came over for the
afternoon. We had a toast. Then darned if she didn't lift
her skirt to reveal a garter between her knee and largest
varicose vein. I tried to split when Henry peeled it off, but
he tossed it clear over the old geezers, and it hit me right
on the back.

"It don't count unless you catch it," I yelled. I picked it
up and took it with me into the bedroom to roll a joint.

We had cheap champagne and salads the gals brought
and fried chicken I'd cooked. Granny was high and higher
from the time she got up in the morning, and Henry was
slurring by three, even with his tolerance.

Henry had to sit down when Gran fed him a bite of
cake, one of my best ever, cut and shaped into a dragonfly,
Granny's good-luck insect. She insisted on a butter cream
icing and pastel decorations to look wedding-like, though
dark fudge would have been tastier. I never knew she had
such a streak of tradition in her, but it was all for a good
cause.

The Monday after the wedding we called our insurance
agent, Mr. O'Neal. He was thrilled to add a term life policy
on Henry to our fire, hurricane, and car insurance. We got
the double indemnity for accidental death.

"Wouldn't you like a policy to protect your husband?"
O'Neal asked Gran. "What if you precede him?"

Gran looked at Henry, and he made some kind of fish
mouth or maybe it was a kissy-face, signaling his love,

trying to get her to take out a policy on herself.

"Nope. Can't afford that right now," she said. "Look at him. Not likely I'll beat him to the grave."

The months flew by like they always did, despite Henry even more underfoot, with chores like feeding the cats or changing light bulbs. He could make anything into half a day's project. He did do a nice job caring for the weed patch and helping with the harvest. He never smoked any, which was good. Alcohol was his drug of choice. Here and there, I got my kicks. One day I was watering and turned the hose on him, pretending it was accidental. He laughed. He wasn't a mean drunk.

He'd converted from a street person to a regular homebody overnight, but his drinking didn't let up any. His one trip a day was for "happy hour" down the street at the Bronco Saloon, unless he was running short on pocket money. Then he grabbed a bottle at the Git 'n Split and brought it home. I tried to make sure he always had enough money to spend some time away.

He was generally in his prime on the porch after dinner before he'd go completely under and we'd have to pry him up and send him to bed. He thought he was some kind of comedian, ole Henry, with his off-color jokes from the saloon. He did have some good ones when he was sober enough to get to the punch line.

The night of their first anniversary we were eating apple cobbler with ice cream and sitting in the swing as per usual, and he poked Gran on her bony thigh. "What did Adam say to Eve the first time they met?"

"Don't know," said Gran, already giggling. She was a sucker for a joke.

"Get lost?" I said. My bad attitude had made me the

straight man.

Henry struck a bold pose. "Stand back! I don't know how big this thing is going to get!"

Gran cackled and nearly toppled off the swing, but Henry caught her and held on, and they vibrated together with belly laughs. I was on the plastic chair facing the street, and I rolled my eyes at Gran, so she knew how pathetic it was, but I had to hold back a smile.

A little later Henry passed out next to her on the swing, his head lolling and mouth open. I put my hand on her shoulder and shook my head, looking into her eyes. "I'm glad you're enjoying yourself, but I'm almost to my limit."

"He's not so bad. He does his chores. He even plunged the toilet this morning."

"He was the one plugged it up."

"Be patient. We're doing great with the extra money." She started rocking her shoulders and strumming the air-ukulele and whispered in my ear, "Next year—Don Ho."

I managed to amuse myself a little over the next ten months by making fun of Henry when he wasn't around. Gran usually joined in. After a joke at his expense, we'd "high five" and Gran would whisper, "Double indemnity." We counted the days till our dream vacation and visualized ourselves sitting at a table piled with lobster and pineapple, sipping Mai Tais with umbrellas and cherries, and watching glistening, tan young men and women in skimpy grass skirts dancing by firelight.

Otherwise, Gran seemed to forget why she married Henry in the first place. She quit some of her stories and started watching the Food Network. One day she decided to make Emeril's candied pecan cheesecake and Paula Deen's butter rum pound cake.

Gran had never baked from scratch before, so I helped her. Within a week we had tried both of those recipes, plus a complicated chocolate soufflé and a baked Alaska like the one I made for my husband on our first anniversary, in 1961. Henry was big on complimenting—his one redeeming quality—and Gran became proud of her new skill. When she no longer needed my expertise, I started making my own specialties, like my famous chicken fricassee. Soon I was cooking fancy most nights, roast with potatoes and carrots, lasagna, paella, and barbequed ribs. Once beef stroganoff, but it had a funny taste. Henry was the only one who'd eat it.

In the evening, he would come shuffling into the kitchen after the saloon, sniffing around, swigging on a bottle of beer. "My mouth is watering," he'd say. "I'm the luckiest man on earth."

He was damned lucky, like he said. If we'd been planning on keeping him for the rest of our lives, he would've needed heavy-duty training, but as it was, we just held on instead of making issues of everything. I looked forward to getting up every morning, just to mark another day off my calendar.

At one year and eleven months, it was high time to start the planning. Gran put me off for a week, so I guessed she was having second thoughts. Finally I caught her in her bubble bath while Henry was over at "Happy Hour." We always used to talk this way, me sitting on the toilet lid, her soaking to soften up her calluses, passing a pipe back and forth to relax, but it had been a long time. She didn't try to talk me out of killing him, but I saw the hesitation in her eyes.

She brought up a good point about stealing the car

to run him over. "Why should we add another criminal offense? More chance to get caught. I don't know how to hot wire anyway, do you?"

"No, hadn't thought about it." It was then that I realized the idea had always been on a fantasy level in my mind. We'd never discussed the gory details. Reality sort of snapped me behind the ears—making a living body into a corpse. In fact, Henry had gotten more lively with the two years of good food. We were gonna send him to hell before his scheduled time, not to mention insuring our own damnation, if such a thing existed.

"Yeah, it's heavy," I said, "but we both know many people that died successfully. Henry will manage."

"Successfully?"

"They got through it. If we do it right, we might be saving the old codger years of suffering."

Gran finished lathering her hair and looked at me with the same kind of doubt I felt. I helped her rinse. She sighed. "We gotta figure out our own method instead of copycatting off the news."

"We want our double indemnity."

"What about accidental poisoning?"

"Huh?"

"Cook up some more beef stroganoff, and that should do it." She was trying for a laugh, but it didn't work.

"We gotta go through with it," I said, "after all our plans and dreams. I'll start to hate him. I'll have to move out."

"No, I'm not letting you do that. We just have to get over this hump."

I let out a lungful of air. "Is he allergic to anything?"

"Not that I know of." Gran lifted up her hand and studied her fingers. "I'm turning into a prune."

I snorted because she'd been a prune for twenty years.

"Shut up," she said. We both laughed, but not for long.

"Let's just drown him in the tub."

Gran nodded. "It's quiet, accidental . . . ."

"He's darn near a walking zombie every night, only needs a little nudge."

"Instead of the bed, I'll undress him and get him into the tub—"

"Give him a few more shots until he's really out of it," I said. "You hold him under till the bubbles stop, and we're home free."

"Me?" Gran asked.

"I can't go into the bathroom with him. It's not normal."

"He never took a tub bath in his life—that's the abnormal part."

I stood up to leave. "All right, I'll help you."

"Damn sure you will."

We planned a martini party to celebrate their two-year anniversary, figuring we'd have plenty of witnesses to tell how drunk Henry was. The idea of a party got us to that day without having to think about the rest. We invited the card ladies, made plates of finger sandwiches, a variety of salads, and fresh fruit for dessert, not having the stomach for anything fancy. We both took out cash advances on our Visa cards for the booze and a bartender, knowing we'd get it all back soon. He could testify how many drinks he served Henry, if needed. Granny wore her robin's egg blue wedding suit, but I dressed in nice slacks and a blouse, thinking what had to be done later.

There was way too much food for the number of guests. "Leftovers for the wake," Granny whispered, but I could see she wasn't enjoying her own joke. Neither of us could fake it by then.

Henry was a regular host for a couple of hours, but then he changed into holey shorts and a ragged t-shirt and took to hanging on people's shoulders and breathing into their faces, telling them how great they were and how much he loved Granny. That drove most everybody out early. He was weaving and slurring, so we knew he'd soon be ready for a bath. God knows he needed one. Everybody at the party could testify to that. By the time we closed the front door after the last straggler, Henry was snoring on the La-Z-Boy.

I pushed on his shoulder. "Come on, old boy, time for bath and beddy-bye."

Granny pulled at his arms and tapped his cheek, trying to rouse him enough to get him walking. She did this every night. Finally, he started to mumble and Granny wrestled him to his feet from her side, and I got one shoulder under his other arm. He took some steps and we got momentum going into the bathroom. We decided it would be near impossible to undress him at that point, and slid him right into the tub. I turned on the warm water and added a capful of Mr. Bubble.

"Wha? Huh?" His eyes were half open.

Gran brought a plastic cup of vodka to his lips and he took a big gulp and smiled up at her, a big goofy grin. She held it till he drank it down and then put a rolled towel on the back of the tub and guided his head onto it.

"Nighty-night, hon."

He closed his eyes and his jaw went slack. I was thinking we would cut his clothes off later.

We stood and stared at the water line as it crept to the

base of Henry's neck.

"It's time," I told Gran. I looked into her eyes and saw panic. "You still want to do this, right?"

She took a big breath and let it out slow. "Yeah, Lu, according to plan. It's time to set things straight by you and get the money."

"You want to hold him under, or me?"

"You're the life guard. You know best."

I gulped. "Not really."

There were tears in her eyes.

"If he starts to squirm, help me hold him down. Are you sure you wanna do this?" I hoped my extra gumption wasn't born of deep buried jealousy. Gran's feelings were as important as mine, but I felt sure she'd be happy when the dirty work was over.

She nodded and took hold of his feet.

She pulled as I pushed, and I climbed in on top of him, kneeling with my legs on his forearms. He twitched, but he was easy to hold. "Sweet dreams," I said to the bald spot on top of his head. I meant it.

Soon a string of bubbles from his mouth burbled against my chest. "I think he's about finished."

Gran let out a cry and ran from the room.

I yelled to her, but she didn't answer. I wasn't sure what to do. Henry twitched again, a feeble attempt to move. Then suddenly he surged upward, knocking me sideways so my head hit the wall. His fingernails dug into my thighs. It took all my strength to keep him down. I pushed him hard. His skull cracked on the enamel of the tub, and a swirl of blood spread in the water. He stopped struggling. A busted skull and a big life insurance policy . . . . I'd seen enough *CSI* to panic.

"Gran, Gran? Come here!"

She didn't come. I heard the screen door slam. I had to make a quick decision. I followed my gut and pulled him up. His eyes were closed.

"Gran, Gran!" I pulled the plug to drain the water. I needed to get him breathing again or we were dead meat. I searched for a pulse in his stubbly neck, couldn't find one. I tipped back his jaw, pinched his nose, and sealed my mouth over his. Liquor breath nearly knocked me out. My training was decades old and I'd never had to revive anyone. Being in the tub made it extra hard. I put my arm behind Henry's neck to get the right tilt to open his airway. I gave four breaths and then four pumps below the sternum as best I could. "C'mon Henry. C'mon, cough and spew and open your eyes."

His lungs inflated, and the air I blew into him whooshed back out at me, sour, as it would be, whether he was dead or alive. I kept going.

When the water had drained down to the suds, I got his back flat on the bottom so I could really work. There was a pink tint to the foam trapped between his shoulder and neck. I gave another set of breaths and yelled for Gran while I pumped.

She needed to call 911 before I wore myself out. I yelled again. She didn't answer. I thought up a story, that we were trying to sober him up, and he knocked himself out. That would explain why he was still in his clothes. Maybe. I wiped away the suds with the wet rolled towel that had fallen down and propped him against the side of the tub, in case he came to and puked. I moved as fast as I could with wet feet, through the hall and into the kitchen to grab the phone, thinking that was what Gran would want me to do. I was giving the address when my eyes caught sight of something bright blue, outside, below the window sill.

I leaned closer and saw what I didn't want to see. Granny in her blue suit, face-down in the grass, the calico curled on her back.

"Two ambulances!" I screamed. "We need two ambulances!"

The 911 operator repeated the address.

I dropped the phone, ran outside, and knelt next to Gran. The cat leaped off and I turned Gran over. Her face was gray and the skin on her neck felt cool. I couldn't find a pulse. I tilted her jaw and pinched her nose and got a whiff of martini, but her breath was sweet. Tears ran down my face and dripped onto her frilly white collar. I kept from sobbing because she needed all my air.

The paramedics took forever. I prayed to the Virgin Mary and all my dead family and friends. Prayers that I thought I'd forgot forty years ago rolled through my brain. Finally, I heard the siren and ran to open the front door and brought the two young men straight back to Gran. I sent the third man into the bathroom, even though I figured Henry was a goner.

I got out of the way so they could work on her. They rousted the calico sniffing her face and set up the oxygen. I stood in the doorway and watched.

In seconds, the fellow came running back through the kitchen. "The man's alive," he yelled. He dashed out the front.

I'd wasted my time on Henry, when I should have been saving Gran. She was still out cold.

"Pump her chest!" I yelled.

The paramedic took the clear plastic cup off her nose and mouth. He looked up at me. "I'm sorry, ma'am. She's gone."

I fell to my knees on the grass. "No, Gran! No! Please wake up! Granny!" I took her hand and rubbed it against my cheek. "No, no, no, no, no—"

"Ma'am. Ma'am." The paramedic took Gran's hand from me and placed it at her side, blocking me with his shoulder when I tried to take it again. "Is she your grandmother?" he asked.

I looked at him.

Tuesday was hot for the funeral, but there was no rain. The poker ladies and some people from Gran's old school, and others who saw the obituary, stood there at the grave service, mopping tears and sweating. A big red rose arrangement was already wilting, although the bird of paradise I'd bought still looked fresh. I was on Valium, which worked better than pot, and keeping steady by holding on to Henry's wheelchair. He had nodded off.

Henry could walk, but he fell down a lot, so it was dangerous to let him try. He'd forget how to put one foot in front of the other in the middle of a step. Mostly he seemed dazed and had little memory, short-term or long. The doctors said his brain had suffered from the lack of oxygen in the accident—or was it the concussion they said? Since I wasn't on the insurance policy, nobody got suspicious.

I came to find out, Henry had a policy on Gran after all. There was a funeral benefit and close to ninety thousand bucks left to Henry after that. I guess he talked her into it, and Gran was afraid to tell me because of the extra cost. Now with Henry brain-dead and without

relatives, there was no clear answer on who was in charge
of the estate. To me, I was the logical choice since I owned
half the property, but the law disagreed. The money would
be doled out over the years by the court, as needed for
Henry's care.

When the time came to say the last goodbye, I rolled
Henry close to the casket and pressed some dirt into
his hand and flung it, as if he was tossing it. He was her
husband after all and maybe she loved him.

I stayed on Valium for the next month, watching soap
operas and watering the weed in the backyard, alone
with my memories. I came to realize that those last years
were some of our happiest—crazy, hopeful days when,
unbeknownst to anybody, those rich desserts were sticking
to Gran's arteries.

Henry sat and stared, wherever I parked him. A nurse
paid by Medicare came once a day to bathe and feed him,
but at night I made dinner and we sat in front of the TV
or on the porch. I learned to maneuver his bedpan so not
to make a mess and to get him into bed. I had no plans,
no dreams. Scuba and luaus had lost their appeal for me
without Gran.

Eventually, I heard on the news that Don Ho was dead.
Goodbye, Mr. "Tiny Bubbles." He was due.

Afterword

by Michael Connelly

Now that you've finished reading this book I can tell you the secret truth behind all the stories. Vicki Hendricks didn't write them for you. She wrote them for herself. Yes, they spoke to you, connected with you, made you think about secret and tortured truths. But they weren't written for you. Hendricks wrote them for an audience of one.

The process of reading is a very personal journey. The reader must make both hidden and obvious connections to the story and characters – mostly the characters. With this empathic bond comes the subconscious nod, the tapping into the primordial importance of storytelling as shared experience and knowledge. The reader says, Yes, I get this. This is true. Sometimes I feel this very same way.

It's in our DNA. Humans need stories to connect and relate. But the secret behind the stories is that they don't start out that way. The writer must write, and she must write for herself first. Everybody else has to get in line.

What I mean by this is that writing is a very personal journey. You keep your head down and you write a story that taps into your own primordial soup. It's got to mean something to you before it can ever mean anything to anybody else. You never lick your finger and hold it up to catch the prevailing winds of creativity and commerce. The true winds blow from the inside out.

I tell you all of this because it takes a certain amount of courage to pull this off. To keep your head down, write something, and then hold it up to the world. Most people pin their laundry to a line out back. Writers hang it right out front for the whole neighborhood to see.

These stories are Vicki Hendricks' clothesline. The colors are varied, ranging from bright reds to blacks and grays. There is humor and an uncomfortable silence in the heart of these stories. There is an undeniable lust for connection and need. Tortured souls, bent souls, kindred souls, in all these stories there is an edgy truth that flaps out there in the breeze.

I've been reading Vicki Hendricks' work for a long time. From day one I've been drawn to that edginess, to the mix of hard-boiled sex and the private desolation and despair of people who feel they might be living in the wrong time, if not on the wrong planet. Hendricks is a true stylist. Her words weren't written for me but they get to me. Right up under the rib cage. The author puts herself out there and into every word of every story. She keeps her head down and writes it for herself, in the most courageous way I know.

—Michael Connelly, October 20, 2009

About the Author

Vicki Hendricks is the author of noir novels *Miami Purity, Iguana Love, Voluntary Madness, Sky Blues,* and *Cruel Poetry,* nominated for an Edgar Award in 2008.

In progress is *Fur People,* a love story about animal hoarding and insanity that takes place in the woods of central Florida.

Hendricks lives in Hollywood, Florida, and teaches writing at Broward College. Her plots and settings reflect interests in adventure sports, such as skydiving and scuba, and knowledge of the Florida environment.

CPSIA information can be obtained at www.ICGtesting.com
Printed in the USA
LVOW05s1615150814

399349LV00017B/1101/P

9 780990 536505